PROLOGUE:

Bak challa challa challa, Bak challa challa challa ...

The seventy-two men sat on the ground chanting, cross-legged, thirty-six of them on either side of the well-worn pathway. As always.

Bak challa challa challa, Bak challa challa challa ...

Twin rectangles facing one another, they took their turn, each group of them, one after another, pointing their hands, aiming their arms over the heads of the fellows, throwing out their chant. Relentlessly keeping the eternal sound a familiar constant in the jungle air.

Bak challa challa challa, Bak challa challa challa ...

There was nothing uniform in the physiology of the two groups of men—not really—not beyond the fact they were all males. The seventy-two were of all ages, all sizes. Many of them were bald, or balding, but not all. Some were tattooed, but none in the same fashion, and not many of them. Now, it was true that none of them was over-weight, but that was more a condition of the harsh region in which they lived. The brutal life endured by the seventy-two, as well as all those who helped carry out their holy work, did not allow for gluttony or over-indulgence.

Bak challa challa challa, Bak challa challa challa ...

Throughout the length of every day, and every

1

night, the scenario was the same. Whether the sun was baking the jungle, draining steam out of all living things, or the heaviest of the winter rains were darkening the skies and drenching all beneath them, during each and every minute, seventy-two men, thirty-six to a group, sat on either side of the mountainous jungle trail, and chanted their holy words.

They did not do so in a rote, or bored, manner. The focus of their entire will was funneled by them, thrown into their sacred work, aimed at the heavens, at those they needed to hear their proffered prayer for the good of all.

Bak challa challa challa, Bak challa challa challa ...

The seventy-two present within the sacred spot were not the only ones who performed their duty. Such would be impossible. The job was supremely tiring—overwhelmingly exhausting. Arms raised to the sky for hours on end, held out-right—rigid. Their focus—unwavering. Their concentration—unbreakable. None could endure such rigors for long.

Several hundred men were part of the same team. Had been for centuries—those who were chosen to perform as the seventy-two. An honor to be selected, they were of no one people. For centuries the honored had been sent from hundreds of different tribes throughout the length and breadth of the continent. At least a hundred were always present at the sacred spot.

Every minute of every day.

Bak challa challa challa, Bak challa challa challa ...

KOLCHAK
AND
THE LOST WORLD

By: C.J. Henderson

To Erik —
Enjoy!

visit us on the web at:
www.moonstonebooks.com

Those not seated studied their fellows on the ground, those performing the rite which must never cease. If they saw one of their number growing tired, beginning to show fatigue, they would carefully walk in between the rows, coming up behind the one they meant to relieve. A simple tap on the shoulder would alert the man on the ground that he was being replaced.

Such judgments were never questioned. There was no shame in giving one's place to another. The Continuing of the Holy Words was not a job. It was not an honor. Not a responsibility or duty. It was all that mattered. It simply—

Was.

Bak challa challa challa, Bak challa challa challa ...

Others guarded those chanting from anything which might interrupt their sacred work. The jungle was filled with predators, but they were the least of anyone's worries. A mountain leopard was not likely to attack a group of such a size. Carnivores were not all that might distract, however. A mischievous simian hurling a nut or stone, striking one of the seventy-two in the eye at the wrong moment, might cause untold damage. A column of biting, mindless army ants, a falling tree, lightning, a burst appendix—those who watched—waiting their turn—never knew how they might be tested, only that every day was merely another to simply be survived.

Bak challa challa challa, Bak challa challa challa ...

Oddly, there was no longer a single living person

3

who knew exactly why the seventy-two did what they did. There were no high priests to tell the tale, no scrolls or clay tables passed down through the millennia to tell the tale. It was simply known and accepted that the sacred chanting was something that simply *had* to be done. That the chanting could not be allowed to stop. Not for a moment.

Not by even a single member of the seventy-two.

Bak challa challa challa, Bak challa challa challa ...

The chanting could not be allowed to cease, for it gave the seventy-two the power to turn any that might wish to pass them—any who might want to go further down the pathway. That much, they knew, could not be allowed. The path only traveled a few dozen feet further, then ended at the base of a wall of basalt and granite. At the entrance to a cavern.

A cavern none must ever enter.

The seventy-two were the guardians of this doorway, their duty to keep anyone or anything that might approach from continuing onward. Such had been the way of those who accepted the responsibility for longer than anyone could remember. Never once over all the centuries they and their countless ancestors had guarded the walkway had they failed.

They would soon, however.

And the world would be thrown into chaos when they did.

CHAPTER ONE:

On March twenty-first, at approximately nine-thirty in the all too early AM, I was informed that I was going to be honored by my peers. The caller laughed when I complained about the detestable earliness of the hour, explaining that rudely shattering the calm of my desperately needed slumber was part of the gag—the good natured joking of comrades. When I asked why he hadn't called even earlier then, he answered;

"Hey, the idea is to inconvenience you—not me. Good God, Carl, what gives you the idea that _I_ would want to be up any earlier than this? Anyway, tomorrow night, The Happy Dragon—6:00—at least for starters. Be prepared for people to buy you drinks and lie to you about how great a reporter you are."

The caller was Ron Shibley, a reporter on the _Gazette,_ and although it pains me to admit it, not a bad guy, actually. My name is Carl Kolchak; I'm a reporter, too, just not a respectable one like Shibley. I work for _The Hollywood Dispatch,_ not the noblest representative the fourth estate had to offer any more. On the other hand, it was still in business in the face of cable news and internet blogs and Jon Stewart and everything else that had swept into town since the turn of the century in its attempt to render the daily newspaper as obsolete as praying before a meal or trusting one's elected officials.

Back in the day I took home my paychecks from some of the biggest news outlets there were, but that was before my moronically idealistic nature got me on the wrong side of some very powerful people who apparently never received the memo that crime doesn't pay. The long and short of it is that they're all still very powerful, uninformed people, while I became a pariah unable to get a job at any A-String paper.

Of course, I didn't immediately descend all the way to the *Dispatch.* No, sending my career into that kind of free fall took some real talent on my part. In between the long ago there and my current now, I found myself working as hard as I could at keeping my mouth shut at a not overly depressing gig in Las Vegas. While there, I had the great misfortune to be the only person from one end of the desert to the other who could manage enough basic arithmetic to put together the various twos lying about into the fairly obviously four that a vampire was thinning the local herd.

Long story short, I annoyed the authorities with this unfortunate truth until I proved my case, was forced by said authorities to dispatch the monster myself, and then was run out of town with a warning never to return for having done so. I've been led to believe in my time that the ancient Greeks treated their monster-slaying heroes with a bit more respect, but then in five thousand years their entire country's never been able to field one decent football team, so what did they know—right?

Over the years since Vegas, I've continued to run into one weird bit of nonsense after another. Not that I've wanted to. Every time I file a story that has the words "witch cult," or "swamp creature," or "headless biker demon from Hell" somewhere in the text, all I do is get another round of finger-pointing started as everyone takes turns telling their latest "oh, that poor demented Kolchak sap" story.

Except that day, that day, for once, was different. True, everyone was excited because I had stopped another monster, but this time it was the more socially acceptable kind of monster—one they could believe in without worrying someone might call them names or start looking for their butterfly net. A serial killer had been hunting through the streets of Hollywood, and my beloved editor, Tony Vincenzo, had decided that since creatures of the night were my specialty, I should cover the story. Vincenzo is a round sort of man, a small, dried-out Brooklyn-born Sicilian, one God placed in this world to help prepare the rest of us for the afterlife by making the thought of death not so unpleasant.

Surprisingly, for once things worked out for me despite Destiny's plan to see me constantly looked upon as the universe's trash basket. Studying the clues at hand, I actually managed to figure out who the happiest gay town on earth's newest headline-grabbing murderer was. Unfortunately, I figured it out while talking to him. And he knew it.

In most cases this might have been the end of the line. But, somehow my luck was still holding. This particular blood-letting lunatic wasn't a stereotypical movie murderer. He was just a guy in his late twenties, a fellow for whom life just hadn't worked out. Being a reporter, I used what meager skills I had to get him talking, to tell me why he was doing what he was doing. Turns out I was in no danger at all. He was so grateful for someone that wanted to listen to him—that was willing to at least try and understand instead of merely dismissing him—he not only told me his life story, but let me record the whole thing as well.

He blubbered and cried less than most would think. A lot of it was over the horror of what he'd done to himself. As he talked to me, about his childhood, of never having success with women, of fearing rejection, dealing with his domineering mother, I could hear in his voice how he was putting it all together for himself for the first time. It was a picture he didn't want to look at. But then, well, who would?

Anyway, what I'm saying is, I was lucky. I didn't try to kid anybody, or make a big deal out of what happened. From the beginning, when I went with him to the police station to help him turn himself in, I said I was just in the right place at the right time. I didn't say anything melodramatic like "I was lucky to be alive," because I wasn't.

Denny Bott wouldn't have tried to kill me if I didn't out-think him or anything like that. There was no movie-of-the-week nonsense tied to what happened. He was tired of what he'd started and was looking for someone to treat him with enough kindness that he'd feel safe confessing to them. He was a sad, confused, lonely guy, and that was about all there was to it.

But, as Carl Denham said, "the public, God bless 'em," they love a hero, and they'll cobble one together from the thinnest materials if they have to. Hell, I've done it myself on a few slow news days—we all have. So, I told myself, okay ... why not? I was lucky enough to be in the right place at the right time. I did my job and was rewarded by Fate for doing so—for once. Didn't I have the right to enjoy it like anyone else?

Anyway, the end result was that the *Dispatch* got to break the story. First photos, first interview, complete confession—everything anyone could want. It sold papers, brought in ad revenue, and earned me enough points with the publisher that I had the feeling he might remember my name at some time other than when he was in a bad mood and needed something to hate.

So, as a reward, a kind of welcoming-back-to-the-fold, a group of local L.A. news types were gathering to take me on a bar crawl of the last-liver-standing variety. I was sure Shibley had started the ball rolling. He was an okay sort, the kind of guy who—although getting paid a lot more than me at a much better outlet for doing basically the same work, but not any better at doing so, if I do say so myself—when he talked to me didn't try to make me feel as if God had gifted

9

me some kind of personal miracle.

I actually debated for a short while as to what I should wear. On the one hand, it probably didn't hurt to dress for success once in a while. On the other, I had no illusions that I was ever going to be offered a better job because I'd worn a cobalt suit on the day that blue became the new brown. On the third hand, I didn't see any point in purposely offending people who might honestly just want to congratulate me on not getting my throat cut by showing up looking as if Ellis Island had been my first glimpse of the new world, either.

In the end, I decided to simply have the better of my two seersuckers cleaned so I might attend this particular clambake as a fairly respectable version of my usual self. And, that decision is what put me within the intersection of two very nondescript Hollywood streets, at 11:15 in the AM on the twenty-third, heading for my very nondescript dry cleaners.

Feeling reasonably pleased with myself, actually smiling as I moved along the boulevard, I did not notice the man approaching me. The one who would try so very hard to warn me of what was coming. Who would struggle to explain to me that which I was not prepared to understand.

And who would subsequently die because of my shortcomings.

CHAPTER TWO:

"You are the Kolchak—yes?"

The fellow was not all that odd, not for the wilds of North Hollywood, anyway. He was, basically, a monk. Not the Middle Ages, sack cloth and ashes, illuminating manuscripts type of monk, but more the shaved head, free Tibet, Richard Gere-loves-ya kind. He was dressed in red and yellow silks, wearing black flip flops. He was also clean shaven—face and head. Like I said, nothing that would stand out in the Martian landscape that was, sadly, my newest home town.

"Yes indeed, it is I, Mrs. Kolchak's darling baby boy, at your service. What's up, my fine fellow?"

I will admit that a part of my brain was wondering who the low rent Dali lama before me was, as well as how he happened to know I was "the Kolchak." I'm not saying that I feel my good mood that morning was putting me in any kind of danger. There was nothing threatening or even off-putting about the guy. No hints of trouble, no "bad vibes" as they said way back when. He simply struck a warning note on the unusual harpsichord, and my radar was making certain I paid a bit of attention. When he spoke again, I will admit I started paying a touch more heed.

"I would ... request you come with me."

"No can do, amigo," I told him, slightly con-

11

cerned with what was going on, but admittedly far more focused on getting my suit home and on and an evening's worth of free drinks inside me than anything else. Giving him a cheerful, but dismissive smile, I told him;

"Unbelievably, for once, I've got things to do. Places to go. People to see—that I actually *want* to do and go and go and see. So, maybe some other day."

I went to keep walking, dismissing the monk as just another typical bit of Hollywood strange, when he reached out and touched my arm as I passed, saying;

"Please, I must ... insist."

I stopped, finally giving the fellow a true scrutiny. There was nothing that came to me in that more intense scan that contradicted my initial reading of him. He was, as best I could tell, a friendly, harmless chap. He was not carrying a weapon anywhere in his robes, of that I was certain. He was not trying to sell me something, did not have anything in the way of evil intentions. If I knew anything about people at all, I knew this simple quiet man was honest, sincere, and in all probability incapable of duplicity.

"Insist?"

I quoted him, stalling for time, failing on all levels to understand what was happening. He was not exuding any of the fear or excitement or confusion, et cetera, that would make me think he was the lead to a story. There was also nothing about him that made me think he represented the beginnings of some sort

12

of con, or in any way wanted to take advantage of me. If he hadn't known my name, I would have moved on without a second thought.

But, he had—he had known my name. And he had, when I thought about it, been waiting for me on a street I normally did not travel. Suddenly, my brain was able to make the Herculean effort necessary to shove aside for a moment the thought of downing many Scotches for which others would be paying. Narrowing my eyes, cutting my field of vision until all my senses were utterly focused on the quiet man before me, I said;

"All right, I'll give you this much, you've got my attention. So, why don't we start with a little leveling of the playing field? Who are you?"

"I am called ... in your tongue ... Smile for the Golden Morning."

Oh well, I thought, rolling my eyes slightly, everyone had to be called something. Not worrying about how he might fit all of that on a driver's license, I moved on, asking;

"Sure, fine. All the rest of it then ... why, exactly, do you need to 'insist' I go with you? And *where* exactly is it you need to take me?"

"You must see ... the seventy-two. Important ... you must understand ... the seventy-two, before you meet them." He turned back toward the direction in which he had come, throwing over his shoulder;

"This way. Not far."

As he began to walk away, I found myself greatly

intrigued. Who knew what the seventy-two might be, or why it was important that I see and understand them? The one thing my brain did remind me of was the way one thing often led to another in my business. Crack one drug story, and bang—everyone with a lead on another one suddenly thinks you're the only person in town to talk to. Of course, I didn't think my monk had seventy-two corpses somewhere he wanted me to help him dig up, but there was enough oddness about the situation to make me realize there was a possibility I might profit by extending him at least a fraction of the time of day.

"Not far, you say," I asked.

"Not far," he answered.

"This way?"

"Yes," he pointed, smiling politely, "this way. Not far."

"Well then, MacDuff, lead on."

Lazy a fellow as I am, even I couldn't argue that the distance we covered in the four minutes and some seconds we traveled was all that far. And, in many ways, the journey proved to certainly be worth the trouble. When Smiley finally stopped, directing me with hand motions to go up a set of carved slate stairs; it was in front of what appeared to be an actual Buddhist temple, there in the middle of North Hollywood.

"We are arrived."

Its windows were decorated with delicate teak wood carvings, lattices depicting intricate scenes—a large finned fish moving through water teeming with frogs, the full moon in a cloudy sky dotted with birds, and so forth. The stone used to put up the building was not necessarily exotic—merely different from the poured concrete and cinder block construction that abounded throughout most of the rest of the neighborhood. It was, oddly, not a place practically anyone would give a second look. But, if they did so, they would find it remarkable in its ability to calm.

"Please ..."

Smiley said the single word, again pointing up the stairs and toward the front door. Figuring if I'd come that far, what was the difference, I accepted his offer and went up the short flight, waiting for my host to usher me inside. He pushed on the unlocked door, sending it open, then bowed slightly, waiting for me to enter.

When I did, I won't say I was startled by what I saw ... I'd have to say I was more impressed. The interior of the single storied building consisted of one large room. There was a simple kitchen along one wall, and a series of bunks along its opposite—several of them occupied. A single door in the back led to what I hoped for the occupants' sake, those awake and asleep, was a bathroom.

In the center of the room, however, things got more dramatic. On a fairly sizeable table, one covered with several immense slabs of what appeared to be marble, cut a half-an-inch thick, there stood a rectangle of candles, all the same size, all the same color, all blazing away. Standing around the table were three men dressed in similar robes to my guide.

Each of them held a long wick. Each of them had a score or so unlit candles positioned in front of them outside of the rectangle of lit ones. None of them paid us the slightest attention as we drew closer. They all simply stared at the dozens of tiny lights blazing in the center of the room. After around a minute of silence, I asked;

"So, you guys ... what? You like to burn candles?"

"They are ... seventy-two," said my guide. "They must burn. Always."

"Or what?"

"That is ... not known."

My guide looked at me with the patience of a guy who really loves his dog, trying to get the mutt to roll over for the thousandth time. Opening his eyes wide, he tilted his head at an angle, first toward me, then toward the candles, asking;

"Do you understand?"

"What, huh? No—understand what? What do you mean," I asked him, no longer thinking I had any idea what was going on. Holding my hands out open before the monk, trying to get across my growing confusion, I asked, "Do I understand *what*?"

"The seventy-two ... do you understand?"

The serenity never wavered. The unwrinkled, patient face never glowered. There was no doubt this fellow thought he was showing me something very important. I hear Congress feels that way every time CNN runs footage of them.

"Must always be lit. The seventy-two."

At this point I began to edge back toward the front door. I figured seventy-two was the number of candles on the table, but what Smiley wanted me to grok after that was something I couldn't fathom. Maybe I was too impressed with myself at that moment, too eager to get on to my evening of many Scotches, or maybe we simply didn't have enough common ground between us to relate.

"Must always *be* ... the seventy-two."

Still nodding, still pointing, he took up one of the yard long wicks and began moving it from candle to candle—testing, stirring. Moving his free hand gently through the air above the blazing rectangle, he smiled as he said once more—

"The seventy-two ..."

Deciding there was no story to be found there, even if the building was North Hollywood's only Buddhist temple, I gave my guide the best smile I could in return, moving myself toward the door, tipping my hat in the general direction of his bonfire—

"Must always be."

And then I was gone.

CHAPTER THREE:

"So Carl, can we throw a party for one of our own, or can't we?"

"Ron," I admitted, always willing to be charmingly gracious when it was someone else's twenties filling my glass, "I say here and now, with my most sincere humility, you gentlemen are the finest congregation of heroes unparalleled it has ever been my pleasure to meet."

Shibley and I clanked glasses over that one. Then, as he and the others began to drink, I stopped my glass an inch from my lips and said;

"Of course, I'm pretty drunk ... so what do I know?"

It was a cheap shot, but it got enough laughs to afford me the opportunity to take a seated bow. It even got a partial spit-take out of my loving boss, Vincenzo, which, although he managed to sprinkle one sleeve of my newly cleaned suit jacket, was worth the price.

Earlier, I had not said "ladies and gentlemen" because, although nearly twenty-five percent of our group had been of the female persuasion when we had started out several hours earlier, the last of them had called it a night three bars back. Which as far as we remaining were concerned was all for the best.

Don't get me wrong, although one of the four of us still drinking the night away, Martey Logan, was as interested in women as I was in learning how to dance with horses, newsmen on the whole are a group fairly well obsessed with the opposite sex. However, leaving the women behind meant we could hit some taverns more geared toward our needs at the moment—places where they were more concerned with keeping the peanuts flowing than the tablecloths clean. Where we could smoke cigars and tell our favorite lies and generally carry on like the nincompoops all guys are underneath, no matter whose photo it is they're looking at when they read a magazine one-handed.

"So, Tony," asked Shibley, his tone surprising me by sliding down into a range more suited to business than shenanigans, "what exactly are your plans for our boy here, I mean, now that he's the big hero of the moment and all?" I protested a slight bit, determined to add modesty to my growing list of positive attributes, but Vincenzo cut me off, slapping me on the back soundly as he answered;

"What am I going to do with our delightful Carl Kolchak, now that, Ron, of the *Gazette*, ummm, now that he is, as you so ... ah, oh ... what's that word, ah ... Carl, what's a good word for 'succinctly?'"

"Ah, another soused Italian," I chimed in, "just what the world needed. 'Succinctly' is probably the best word you'll find, Tony."

"Thanks, Carl," answered Vincenzo. He was smil-

19

ing so widely as he did so I wondered exactly what they'd been putting in his drinks, and if I could get away with spiking the water cooler at the *Dispatch* with some. Turning back to Shibley, still grinning, he said;

"Since as you put it so ….succinctly—yes, that is a good word, Carl, thank you—-ummmm … now that he is now a hero, I have to admit, I haven't quite figured out what assignment I'd like to have him handle next." Looking upward toward the ceiling, his eyes affecting a near-statesman-like quality, he mused;

"What, indeed, would be a worthy way to exploit our star reporter's newfound fame … since it appears it might be enough to make people forget about all his crazy nonsense from the past."

I covered my face with one hand, muffling a groan as Vincenzo started rattling off his laundry list of my favorite stories.

""Cruise Ship Carnivore,' that's always been one of my favorites. Or that one about the microbes that ate people … and the aliens, don't forget them—*any* of them. Or—"

Vincenzo's list of my greatest hits was interrupted by a belch that caught him unawares, an intrusion so boisterous; it knocked him backward along with his chair several inches. Indeed, by the time he recovered, he'd forgotten the topic of conversation. He did, however, force himself to his feet to take a bow when Shibley and Logan broke out in applauds for his impromptu serenade. Despite the others' enthusiastic calls for an encore, however, my beloved editor decided to rest on his laurels—at least for the moment. Which, it turned out, was what Shibley had been waiting for.

"I actually had a reason for asking what I did, Tony," he announced to the table. "Martey here is in on this already. I did wait for the others to take off first, but—"

"Now that they're gone ..."

"Yeah," he answered me, a twinkle in his eye I had to admit had me more than a little intrigued, "now that they're gone, I have a proposition for you."

"My star reporter is not that kind of girl."

Logan's horse laugh at Vincenzo's comment was so loud it turned most of the heads in the bar, prompting my growing-less-lovable-by-the-minute editor to push himself upward for another bow. Sighing, but working at keeping a sure-I-can-take-a-joke smile plastered on my face, I asked;

"Before you give the ambassador from Sicily here a heart attack, could we get on with this? I mean, a young thing like me needs his beauty rest."

This comment led to mounds of ridicule, of course, but it also pushed things over the top enough that everyone involved was willing to be serious for at least a few moments. Taking charge of the conversation once more, Shibley said;

"Okay, I assume everyone here is aware that south of the border there is all manner of drug violence going on—yes?" Once we all agreed he was correct, the rising young star of the *Gazette* continued, saying;

"There's one conflict going on now in the mountains of Columbia that's shaping up to be a real beauty. It's tearing along in the Andes, back and forth across Columbia's border with Ecuador."

"Haven't heard anything about this," I admitted, hating to do so, but knowing it was for the best.

"Makes sense, since nobody has. The State department's been keeping the lid screwed down tight on this one. But, it's about to blow."

"How so," asked Vincenzo, the smell of a story burning away the vapors of his drunk. Already halfway to sober, he followed up his vague question with a more direct one;

"And, how is it you know about it?"

"You see, guys," quipped Shibley, "that inquiring mind ... that's why he gets to sit behind a desk and we have to work for a living." When Vincenzo's eyes narrowed slightly, Shibley made a joking apology, and then got back down to business.

"Two rival production gangs are slugging it out, and apparently the violence is getting out of control. Because of the way the drug battles in Mexico are drawing so much attention, these two are working at knocking each other out of the picture. Having only one supplier in that area would ramp down the price wars, throw a little stability up to Mexico; help straighten everything out down there."

"And ..."

"And, Mr. Vincenzo," offered Shibley with a smile, "as is the way of self-interested politics, State doesn't want to see things calmed down. I've got a contact there, a perfectly charming fellow always willing to risk my neck to push forward his own agenda. He's cued me to this because he thinks it's in State's best interests if the American public gets wind of this."

"More death for the front pages," I guessed aloud. "Draws more negative attention to the whole region, helps keep things destabilized, makes it easier for us to send in troops at their governments' request ... something along those lines?"

Shibley made a gun out of his hand, shooting me with his forefinger as he said;

"Bingo. Officially, the president's made pacts with the heads of the involved nations to keep things quiet so the violence might cool down a bit. But, that means an uninterrupted flow of drugs into America, at cheaper prices."

"So," offered Tony, "this leak allows for public outrage, and thus the president has no choice but to go back to business as usual. Tidy. What's all this have to do with Carl?"

I liked watching my prune of an editor work. Seeing him do it once in a while reminded me as to why I had ever afforded him any respect in the first place. Tipping a non-existent hat to Vincenzo, Shibley said;

"I want to take him with me. We would fly into Ecuador, make our way into the Andes, get interviews with members of both sides, snap some photos, make big promises about playing up how they should be in charge of their countries because their governments are so corrupt ... the usual piffle. While they hopefully believe us, we send our stories back, and then zoom the hell out before they get their asses handed to them by a coalition built from our Marines working with the Ecuadorian and Colombian forces."

Questions flew from Vincenzo and I both after that, some of which Shibley handled, some by Logan. It seemed that our government severely wanted U.S.-friendly coverage to break in the States before they sent in the troops. It was, as usual, more a thing of timing so political points could be racked up by the current administration before the next election. That doing so might save lives, or stem some of the unbelievable violence that was spilling over the southern border of our country from Mexico, or turn a bit of the seemingly never-ending tide of cocaine and other substances flooding the U.S. were nothing more than perks to our elected officials, apparently. But, the truth of the matter was, those in State making Shibley aware of this were far more concerned with their own agenda than worrying about how much blood was spilled in places they had no intention on visiting.

They were so interested in making this happen that they had already provided Shibley with the necessary paperwork, passports, and travel arrangements. Plane tickets had been bought, hotel rooms secured, guides and vehicles hired. They had even helped my old pal pick the crew that would go.

Shibley was a media star—young, handsome, and the top player at his paper, all reasons State kept him in their contact files in the first place. Both black and gay, Logan was a politically correct double win. He admitted he was not terribly flattered with making the cut that way, but that it was that kind of world and he was fairly used to it by that point. One of the ladies who had dropped out of our cross-town alcohol quest, Marsha Bernstein, had been included because, as Logan quoted her as having put it;

"Who needs a degree from Berkeley and three different UPI awards when you've got both a vagina *and* a taste for Mogan David?"

Which left me.

"So," I asked, bile and sarcasm fighting to color my words, "considering all that, what exactly is it I bring to the table that the State department finds me worth wasting tax payer dollars on?"

"Are you kidding," asked Shibley. Signalling our waiter to bring another round, he said, "You're our team leader."

"Do tell ... and how does that work?"

At this point my old pal put his hand up, making a motion that we needed to watch what we said from that point forward, indicating that we had to be careful not to be overheard.

"The whole thing's been arranged under the cover that we're not going in to expose this drug war ... we're going in to investigate the rumors that the violence might spill over into a sacred site there in the mountains."

And suddenly, all was made clear. This wasn't an offer being made to a newsman, my paranoid side noted bitterly. No one wanted me along because of my body of work, or even to exploit my newfound status as a hero, such as it was. No, it was a calling in of the tinfoil-hatted crackpot. Hell, the bozos at State probably thought having me along made everyone else safer, since not even drug warlords would take anything seriously as a threat if Kolchak the nut job was involved.

I have to admit, at that moment I was suddenly not in a very good mood. What had seemed for a moment as the barest beginnings of a chance to get my life back to something resembling normalcy, had turned out to be just another horse laugh aimed in my direction—Carl Kolchak, the idiot who believes in vampires. Yeah, get him. Hell, even if he dies, who would possibly care?

My mind went red at the idea, overwhelmed with such a level of anger that at first I couldn't even come up with a response. A sliver of me noted that Logan was hearing about this part for the first time, and that he might not be particularly happy about it. I also noticed that Vincenzo had gone silent, indicating that he understood my mood and was leaving any decision up to me. Still, I found it more than a little difficult to rein in my anger. Allowing a trickle of the lava choking me to spill over the rim, I asked;

"Yeah, a sacred site. Call in the hoodoo expert. Take the dancing monkey along. He's good for a laugh. He knows about every bit of Bermuda triangling, pyramid-powered crap in the universe. Christ, Ron ... what the hell kind of sacred site could there be down there in the middle of all that mess anyway?"

Shibley pulled in on himself for a moment, a look spreading across his face that suggested he had come across something which might have upset his belief in something else. Leaning in conspiratorially, he whispered;

"Carl, have you ever heard of ... the seventy-two?"

And suddenly, at that moment, as my blood froze and the words "why me" came unbidden to my lips, I knew no amount of alcohol existed to get me as drunk as I wished I could be.

CHAPTER FOUR:

Only sixteen hours after my little, less-than-sincere congratulations party had broken up, Shibley, Logan, Bernstein and myself found ourselves sitting in our business class seats, working out exactly how we expected to live through the insanity we had accepted into our lives. And, trust me; words being my business, "insanity" was one I chose as carefully as I do the rest.

For some reason, when Shibley had asked if I'd ever heard of "the seventy-two," I did not tell him about my encounter with Smile for the Golden Morning. Maybe I wanted an ace up my sleeve. Maybe I wanted to hear what he had to say first. Most likely I was too snockered to think the connection was worth mentioning. So, when I simply stared at him, he launched into the smattering of facts he had.

Somewhere in the midst of where the drug warlords were slaughtering one another, rumor had it there was a hidden city, a second Machu Picchu, or whatever. Shibley said the stories about the city were wildly random, dating back at least four hundred years. However, no matter how dissimilar they were, most of these stories mentioned this "seventy-two," a something-or-other that needed to remain there unmolested to perform some important task.

To his credit, Shibley didn't seem to consider us on some sort of holy crusade. His feeling was that if there was some sort of temple or ruins or whatever there in the middle of this conflict, that would give our story an edge—like when the extremist Muslims in Afghanistan had started destroying art treasures that weren't acceptable to their religion. As he had put it;

"People are jaded, Carl. Drug dealers kill people all the time. You can't sell papers with the slaughter of the innocent any more. People are just too used to it, and too overwhelmed by it. There's gotta be something more ... something to jazz it up. Am I right?"

Of course, he was. It was a sad commentary on our modern society, but an honest one. The public hears about death and merely shrugs their collective shoulders. They can accept it, because it happens to everyone, and with the world population crawling quickly along toward seven billion, a part of their minds doesn't see anything wrong with a bit of murder—as long as it's not in their neighborhood.

But, the destruction of art treasures, the wanton elimination of one-of-a-kinds, that gets a certain segment of the population howling. Also, I had to admit it was a lucky break for all of us that Shibley'd stumbled across this angle, because it really appeared as if things were working for all of us. To be fair, this deal was looking pretty sweet for all included.

All our outlets would have complete access to everything that any of us sent back. Vincenzo, as well as his and my lords and masters back at the *Dispatch*, were ecstatic. So much money had been poured in to financing our trip from television sources putting the grab on whatever images we generated, that the paper was getting away with a total cost of no more than paying my salary while I was out of town. As Vincenzo put it, the paper was in for an equal share of a major story and all they had to do what not have me around for a week or two.

"Stay a month," he had said as I left his office earlier that morning, "make all of Los Angeles happy."

Sometimes I wonder exactly what it is that rolls around within my sainted Sicilian's head instead of brains. Half the time he's screaming from the rooftops over the stories I hand in, conveniently forgetting that he was the one that handed me the assignment I was reporting on in the first place. Was it my fault every time I turned around some disembodied thing or whatever was crawling up out of its grave and wandering into whatever it was I was trying to report on?

But then, after reading me enumerable riot acts about covering the odd or weird or what have you, he purposely sends me on assignments like this one, suddenly not caring if Big Foot or Atlantis or Spring-Heel Jack was involved, as long as it meant he'd get copy people would plunk down their change for, copy that would bring in readers, which would boost ad sales, which would keep the revenue trickle going long enough for us all to draw another pay check.

I'm not sure if I'm complaining about the man or

not. I think more, at that moment on the plane, I was bitching about how Fate considered me nothing more than her rag doll. Although most don't believe it when I say it, in all my career I have never tried to find a supernatural angle within any story. After Las Vegas had delivered unto me undeniable proof that such angles did indeed exist—subsequently destroying what was left of my ability to be a serious newsman—I tried even harder to not find any supernatural angles within any story.

And yet, there I was, being flown off to a remote corner of the world because I had the knack for finding such angles—with Vincenzo's blessing, no less. It was that kind of reality that made me glad they still allowed drinking on planes. Not that I was in the mood to knock anything back after the night before, but I was happy to know the option was available.

"Hey, Carl," asked Shibley, "mind if I give you a bit of advice?" When I told him to feel free, he did so, asking me;

"Have you ever considered *not* fighting the fame trying to make you into a celebrity?"

"I'm sorry," I answered, wondering where he was going with such a statement, "I thought you were talking to me. Forgive me for interrupting your conversation with whomever this other 'Carl' is."

"Meaning...?"

"Meaning what the hell are you talking about? Celebrity? You know, when you're going to yank someone's chain, you really should start from a premise they at least have a tiny chance of believing. That's how you draw them in."

Shibley sighed like a father who has explained tying one's shoe to his ten year old for the ten thousandth time and was now bordering on simply punching the little doof in the head. Playing the part of the little doof, I was not pleased, but I was beginning to wonder why I seemed to do this to everyone. Turning to our companions across the aisle, he pleaded for assistance. Logan and Bernstein pretended to flip a coin, Ms. Bernstein groaning in mock horror when she was elected by Fate to deal with me. Fixing me with her, I had to admit, very nicely colored green eyes, she said;

"Look, Carl ... I think what Ron is getting at is that ... yes, in the opinion of the old school, you're a failure. We won't argue with you that the dinosaurs in our business, and plenty of others, see you only as a trouble-making kook—savvy?"

"Yes, ma'am," I told her, pitching my voice as young as I could.

"Your problem is, you were born just when things were beginning to change. So, you were brought up in a dying culture. Sure, the elite doesn't want to hear from vampires and UFOs and the such, but the sub-culture does—big time. And, in case you didn't know it, the old school is dying off, and the sub-culture is taking over."

While Bernstein continued to lecture me on what the youth culture was tuned into and who some of their unlikely heroes were, Logan had begun typing away on some kind of electronic gizmo I didn't recognize. Don't get me wrong, I love my computer—anyone that would still work on a typewriter these days would have to be insane—but I haven't even begun to cross over into the world of I-phones and pads and tweets and all the rest. Urging Bernstein to switch seats with me, Logan motioned me over, demanding;

"C'mon, old timer, time for an education."

"Old timer," I bristled with pretend anger. "I'm not even forty, you cupcake."

"Yeah," my impromptu teacher interrupted, "but you act like you were born in the fifties. Now sit down and let me show you a few websites you might not have come across in your nightly search surfing spots like hotchicks.com."

For almost an hour Logan showed me scores of sites from all around the internet dedicated to the occult, the supernatural and the just plain goofy. A number of them were quite scholarly, in their own way—several attached to universities. I have to admit, the one for Duke University impressed me pretty much, but that was because even I'd heard about the two professors from that school who seemed to run into almost as much oddball stuff as myself.

As far as the random sites went, the fact that my name came up in many of them, listing me as an authority on this and that, did not actually surprise me. I had met a fellow named Larry a while back, proprietor of a pretty terrific little home-style restaurant named Let Larry Feed Ya. He was a bit of a self-taught expert on the weird, and had been the first to lecture me on my growing notoriety. The way my fellow reporters were all rallying behind me there in the plane brought all his positive attitude back to me. Throwing my hands up, I admitted;

"All right, okay, enough. You all win. I'll ... I'll think about it. Fair enough?" My companions all looked one to the other, smiling in triumph. Finally, Shibley said;

"I've known this grumpy old fossil a long time. I think that's the best we're going to get out of him. Besides—"

He pointed up toward the FASTEN SEATBELTS signs which had started blinking over all our heads.

"Looks like we're going to be coming in for a landing."

Bernstein and I did not bother to switch back to our original seats. It was no big deal, I thought, until I realized that meant Shibley got to walk off the plane with a very attractive raven-haired looker, and I got to walk off with a gay guy.

"Who," a voice from the back of my mind whispered in a chuckling tone, "is also a very attractive raven-haired looker."

I grinned at the thought, telling myself that if I could make those kinds of jokes, who knew, maybe I was more modern than I thought.

CHAPTER FIVE:

Our flight had gotten us into the airport in Quito, Ecuador, too late to do anything outside of finding our hotel and getting settled in for the night. I got a surprise when we checked in as to our roommate situation. I had been assuming Shibley and I would be sharing one room and Bernstein and Logan the other out of some old fashioned notion of propriety—which made me think that perhaps I wasn't so modern after all.

The surprise came when Bernstein said she wanted to bunk with me, instead. After Shibley made the expected immature alpha male remarks, which I will admit I enjoyed muchly, and Logan did a full diva turn at being wounded by such callousness on his part, Bernstein called a halt to our testosterone-fueled shenanigans by explaining;

"Martey, you're a wonderful human being, but I was at the Clinton Q&A when you fell asleep. You snore louder than rush hour traffic."

"That's half an explanation," said Shibley slyly, "but it doesn't tell us why you chose Carl over me."

"Because from all reports I've got a much better chance of getting a decent night's sleep with him instead of you. And, before you take this any further, decide just how insulted you want to be, because I can find a level to accommodate any amount of mind slap you'd like."

I wish I could say that at least one of the males in our group—professional wordsmiths all—had come up with a pithy rejoinder, but none of us did. Logan, of course, had the least reason to be insulted. It had been years since he had been forced to cover the Clinton speech in question after having pulled a thirty-six hour stake-out on a sting operation. His editor had needed someone and sent out "the new kid" telling him it didn't matter if he even brought back a story— they just needed a body in a seat.

Logan had apparently passed out after forty-two seconds of the Secretary of State's brilliant chatter, and began sawing logs ten seconds after that. Clinton shrewdly labeled him as a republican who obviously couldn't wait until her speech was over to start hurling the red state party-line at her. This had gotten a lot of applauds and laughs, but not enough to wake poor Logan up, which got even more laughs. The poor guy has not even begun to live the whole thing down to this day.

Shibley, of course, had taken a direct hit right between the eyes, but don't make the mistake that Bernstein was implying some sort of romantic overture toward yours truly. To the contrary, her tone got across quite nicely that she considered me utterly harmless, which believe me; even an utterly perfect gentleman does not want to hear.

Regardless, we found our rooms, claimed our

beds, unpacked to whatever degree each of us preferred, then met back in the hotel's dining room for a late dinner. The restaurant wasn't bad at all, considering how little choice we had. Late at night, strange city, in South America, not all that far from a drug war zone—it wasn't like we were going to grab a cab and start roaming Quito for something better. We'd simply come off a long flight, were seriously hungry considering the way the airlines don't feed anyone anymore, and would have gone to a Burger King if it was the closest option available.

The waiter seemed disappointed when we all passed on alcohol any stronger than wine. The truth was, as a group we'd injured ourselves fairly severely back in L.A., including Bernstein who'd left two hours earlier. Considering what we would be heading into in the morning, it seemed prudent to all of us that one bottle of wine split between the four of us be the total of that night's festivities.

Dinner was a house specialty, one with which we were all glad we allowed the waiter to tempt us. It came with as much rice and spinach as one wanted, but the main course was meat—or should I say courses. In near never-ending waves, platters of wonderfully roasted meat were brought to our table from which we got to spear our own portions.

The first was a garlic chicken, roasted crispy, skin intact, and yet still juicy. I noticed where I took a thigh, Bernstein grabbed a trio of wings, Logan a breast and Shibley a leg. I found it interesting that we all liked different parts, but not enough so to make any comments. After the chicken came duck, then quail, and after that there was no time for commentary.

The bird course was followed by pork. Slices of ham were offered first, covered in a glaze that tasted as if it were made from crushed pineapple and mildly hot peppers. Sausages followed that, fat, well-browned links that had been wrapped in bacon. These delights were followed by pork chops, wonderfully browned affairs edged with just enough fat to make every bite delicious.

The next platter brought by was loaded with beef, as expected, in every cut imaginable. The rare slabs were all piled at one end, mediums in the middle, and well done at the other end. Thinking we were at the end of our meal, all of us took a nice sized slab and dug in. Ten minutes later we got a small education in life outside the United States.

Unlike home, many other countries consider fish just another meat—and well, considering the definition of the word, right they are. That simple truth didn't help us, however, when three-quarters of the way through our beef portions we were suddenly presented with everything the sea had to offer. Shrimp large enough to fill the circumference of a coffee cup, fat and steaming and covered in butter, chopped onions and garlic. Large fillets, smothered in mushroom slices, as well as clams, oysters, mussels, fried squid, cold octopus wrapped in thin strips of bread, and other dishes we had to turn back without seeing them out of fear we might eat ourselves into stupors.

When we finally staggered away from the table, the four of us all agreed that none of us could remember the last time we'd eaten so much. Closing in on forty the way I am, I usually make a conscious effort to simply sample everything, but to not overload. Still, by the time the seafood had arrived even I had to surrender. We had been overwhelmed with food, all of it good, some of it perfect. After spending enough time to both pick a point in the AM when we would regroup in the lobby, as well as debating exactly how extravagantly we should over-tip our waiter for suggesting such a marvelous meal—we were on an expense account, after all—we staggered off to our bedrooms for some much needed rest.

I graciously gave Bernstein the first shot at the bathroom. When she tried to be gracious back, I informed her that I was so stuffed it might take me a good half hour to be able to unfasten my belt safely. She responded by letting loose a tremendous belch!, one I had to respond to with applauds as she said;

"There you go, Carl, that's how you make more room."

I promised her I'd make a note of her splendid suggestion, as well as letting her know she was my kind of girl. She gave me a playful curtsey, digging her forefinger into her chin for effect. I nodded in response, and then told her to be on her way. After she was safely behind the closed bathroom door I did immediately loosen my belt and undo my pants, desperately needing that bit of release. I sighed heavily, sinking into the room's single large, stuffed chair. Closing my eyes, I sank into its softness gratefully, happy as I'd been in I could not remember how long. As I simply relaxed, a part of my mind noted that I'd had worse weeks in my time.

Acknowledged as a fearless hero journalist, celebrated by my peers with a deliciously long drinking binge, being rewarded with an, as previously mentioned, expense account-driven international assignment, and then a girdle-buster of a meal, the self-satisfied part of my mind whispered that it could not imagine how things could possibly continue onward so wonderfully.

Smiling, I agreed with myself that for once, things were not going all that bad.

And then, I drifted off into a light slumber, and the nightmare which had been waiting for its chance at me moved in, reminding me as to why I should never expect anything good in my life.

CHAPTER SIX:

The fear struck quickly, my spine going horribly cold because I knew I was in trouble. I was aware that I was dreaming, but for the first time in my life, I had realized that fact while walking across a broad and blasted field. I couldn't tell if it was merely a vast flat expanse, or it was filled with waving grain or blowing sand. Whatever it was, it was simply all around me, blurred in bright scarlet.

Along the horizon beyond the everlasting plane stood mountains, seemingly in all directions. Gigantic, towering purple-hued peaks that were filled with lightning. Seeing that is what was overwhelming my mind with the screaming desire to wake up. Of course, I will explain.

You see, if you have ever heard the old notion that if you die in a dream, you will die in real life, I'm here to tell you ... it's absolutely not true.

At least, not most of the time.

Usually, we go to bed and have our normal little bits of hate and confusion and frustration filtered out of our minds because that is, so the head doctors tell us, the main purpose of dreams. Those who study such things say our nightly flights of fancy are merely our brains attempting to sort out our problems, try-ing to make sense of things, catalogue new information, keeping us alive for whatever reason they can find to justify our continued existence. It's all just a blur of symbolic icons and day-to-day dribble. And not a big deal.

Hell, babies can do it.

But there are places we can wander when we older types dream that babies can't. And wouldn't want to.

There're those who call it the Ether. The near beyond. Purgatory. I've heard it defined as an alternate reality and a parallel dimension. Every culture, every era has had a name for it, but the one I know it best by is the dreamplane. It's a land beyond, a land of the mind that people can reach when they dream. Where they can manipulate the local reality with their minds. Where for all intents and purposes, they can be gods.

If, that is, they know how.

At least, that's what I've been told by a growing number of people who fully believe they've walked it. Waged wars in it. Bent it to their will. Very convincing people.

I tell you all this because I've been warned by the majority of them that the dreamplane was not a place for those not ready to deal with it. It was quite possible for ordinary folks to reach the dreamplane completely by accident—or even to have their minds pulled there by predators—people with absolutely no idea they were in a dream from which they might not awaken. A dream where they could be eaten.

A dream where they could die.

These various purported travelers of the beyond, many of whom did not know each other, have still always given me a fairly consistent description of this place. They would tell me, if I was dreaming and I ever found myself on a flat, sprawling scarlet field, and then I saw a purple mountain range on the horizon, one with lightning striking, that this meant I had reached the dreamplane.

When these folks would tell me about this, fascinated by the consistency of their individual reports, I would always ask them the same question—what comes next? Every single one of them then told me something different.

Not every story of the dreamplane I've heard over the years ended badly. But I knew I hadn't come looking for it, had not wanted to ever visit it. So, if I was there, I had been pulled there—possibly by something as simple as my being in the wrong place at the wrong time, as usual—somehow having ended up in the path of some combination of gravities that caught hold of my thoughts, or maybe by something sinister looking for life forces to feed upon.

I'd been told that one's time on the scarlet plane varied. Some spent days getting somewhere else, for others minutes, hours. Seconds. That's what it was for me. Seconds. I walked in the vermillion haze just long enough for me to realize where I was, and then I wasn't there any more.

There is a natural hope that hits those who have been warned of the dreamplane that it could still simply be a dream. In their waking time they were told of such a thing happening, and then sooner or later they ended up having a dream about going to the dreamplane. A way to feel important. Like convincing oneself they were Cleopatra in another life. Self-fulfilling prophecy. I was told that defense protected no one. Denial worked no better in the near beyond than it did in the waking world.

Warily I tried to get my bearings, to figure out to where I'd dreamed myself. All around me I was met by a big city setting. Evening. Steam coming up out of the sidewalk grates. It was raining, making the scene appear darker than it really was. As I concentrated, I realized I had somehow moved inside, into a Koreatown style grocery, standing in the vegetable section.

For some reason, I had an overwhelming urge to look at the vegetables. To inspect them, row after row. Up and down. Walking in between and around the five, or maybe it was six, white-smocked clerks tending to the produce. The first row I couldn't have named a thing I saw. The first three bins held greens, various broad leaves, but none I recognized. The next four held mushrooms of different varieties, but none of them the familiar little white ones I grew up with. The last two were odd bulb-like things. Why this was important to me, I had no idea.

The next row held vegetables I did recognize. Spinach, broccoli, carrots and then four different kinds and colors of peppers—after that cabbage and then lettuce. Then, the next row took me back to

44

things I'd never seen before.

I wandered the store, up and down the rows, trying to puzzle out what I was doing. After a while, a Korean gentleman I would have guessed to be in his early sixties came up to me, and beckoned to me, as if he wanted me to see something. We walked a few blocks, the drizzle not really heavy enough to be a bother, until we reached another grocery store. It was a different neighborhood, but the store was still Korean.

When we went inside, I didn't see anything all that much different from the place we had left. Aisles of canned and bottled goods. Boxes of tea and noodles and powdered gelatin, odd foreign candies and cookies, et cetera. And the same kind of produce section—the same in that I felt the same overwhelming urge to inspect it.

Once more I walked the aisles, again making my way around the clerks, and again my guide led me back out into the rain and on to another store where I repeated the process. And again at another, and then at another.

How many we saw, I don't know. They simply faded one into another. Finally, however, we reached one which, although no different than any of the others, made me stop for some reason I could not fathom. The back of my mind had noticed something, but I had no idea what it might be.

Making my way in between the various clerks, I once more looked at the contents of the bins, trying to discern some sort of pattern, or message. Or some-thing. Part of my brain kept hammering a singular thought at me, that this was not a simple dream where some showgirl was going to come out and do won-derful things to me, or I was going to fall and fall and never hit bottom, or run slower and slower while something unknown got closer and closer.

That was not the way the dreamplane worked. Where I was, for all intents and purposes, was ab-solutely real. Something had brought me to some kind of somewhere and wanted some kind of result for its effort.

In frustration I studied the fruit row. Five differ-ent kinds of apples. Three of pears. Plums followed. Then, I was around the bend and onto the next row. Fruit once more. Bananas came first, followed by mangos, then those three differently sized things that all look like small oranges. I know one of them is a tangerine, but I don't know which one. Kiwis, peaches, pineapples and plantains. And then I was in another row. And another.

And another and another and another and an-other.

What was I missing? I couldn't figure it out. Not for a minute. And then it hit me.

The clerks, always in motion. Sorting the vegeta-bles and fruit. Cleaning, removing bad leaves, pluck-ing, polishing. Caring for their bins. Keeping them filled. Eight rows of bin in each store.

Eight rows of nine bins apiece.

"The seventy-two," the old man said as the numbers came clear in my mind, "must always be fresh."

All the clerks turned toward me then, their hands continuing to work as they joined the old man in saying;

"The seventy-two must always be."

And then I awoke, maybe twenty minutes after I had first dozed off, sweating, soaked through my shirt and jacket, hoping to god the damn room had a mini-bar.

One with Scotch in it.

CHAPTER SEVEN:

"Carl, are you all right?"

Bernstein, still in the bathroom called to me through the door. Sitting forward, not blinking, mouth dry, I stared at the door for a moment, unable to remember where I was, who it was that had called out to me, why they would do so.

"Carl...?"

I shook my head, slowly at first, then violently, shaking away the last traces of dream, gasping for breath as I tried to force myself to stay awake. I found myself opening and closing my mouth, my tongue sandpapering its way over my parched lips.

"Kolchak, God damn it! What the hell was all that about?"

Blinking my eyes hard, forcing myself to pay attention to Bernstein's voice, I croaked out a typical answer, assuring her that everything was "over" and that I was "fine." She responded by asking if I was so "fine," then what had I been screaming about?

I responded that I had been dreaming. When she answered, sounding a great deal calmer, that it must have been a hell of a dream, I agreed with her, letting her know she had no idea, but that I would explain when she emerged from her evening ablutions. She came out in under thirty seconds, sitting down on her bed with her hair wrapped in one towel, the rest of her wrapped in one not much larger. Looking back on the moment, I find a part of me shocked that I didn't really notice her state of undress. But then, that's the way a guy gets when the world of the strange starts rapping on his door with predictable regularity. Everyday reality, no matter how attractive, simply has to take a back seat.

"So, what in the name of God were you dreaming about?"

"I know this will sound like an odd question," I croaked, my voice raspy and still sounding slightly disoriented, "but ... I was really screaming? Loud? A lot?"

"No, not a lot," she answered, giving me something to be grateful for, "but the one you did give out with was long and yes, really loud, and it scared the crap out of me."

"Sorry about that."

"Apology accepted," she said. Drawing her legs up under herself, she continued, asking, "Now spill. What got the little-girl-noise out of you?"

"I was taken on a tour of Korean grocery stores."

Bernstein fixed me with a look I knew all too well. It was the reporter's scrutiny, the truth-o-meter stare. We can't help ourselves, it's part of any newshound's make-up. Give us something to be suspicious about, and we automatically trip the switch on our bullshit meters. After just a few seconds she switched it off, even though her face's features retained their puzzled arrangement—meaning she might not understand what I was talking about, but at least she believed me.

Clearing my throat once more, trying to clear a path through the unexpected phlegm build-up that had seized me, still not quite able to talk clearly, I was ready to try and explain when she slid off the bed, heading for the bathroom. She told me not to talk, then returned with an open bottle of water. As I stared at it, she explained;

"Brought a few of them for myself, emergency rations, sure. Mostly for brushing my teeth. I've seen dysentery. Now drink, you sound like hell."

I took several small sips, swishing them around in my mouth, gargling slightly each time before swallowing. Handing the bottle back to her, I thanked her, then began again. I told her of my dream, of how it led to the seventy-two. Then I told her of my meeting back in Hollywood with Smile for the Golden Morning. Staring at me, she narrowed her eyes slightly, then asked;

"And when were you going to tell the rest of us about this?"

"Marsha, come on ... I mean, this dream ... that just happened ten seconds ago. As for the monk and his candles, well ... I don't know ... "

"But, what does it *mean*, Carl?"

"What? 'What does it mean?' Why are you asking me?"

Bernstein hadn't gone back to her seat on her bed when she had brought me the water, but had sat on my bed which was closer to the chair. Somehow, the intensity of the moment hid that fact from me, kept me from realizing then just how provocatively she filled out her too-small towel. Leaning forward, closer than either of us realized, she answered;

"It was your dream, Carl. And besides, aren't you the expert on this kind of thing?"

I wanted to protest, to yell "what kind of thing," or "what makes me the expert," or anything that might allow me to turn away from the truth of the matter. To shirk the responsibility she was assuming was mine. I didn't, however, because—at least partially—she was right. It had been my dream. And as far as weird and creepy and scary crap was concerned, yeah, sure, okay—fine—maybe I am the expert. Expert at falling into it, anyway. And, there was one more thing gnawing at me, as well.

My mind flashed on her earlier question of when I was going to tell everyone what I knew. I hadn't really given her any kind of explanation about that yet, but that wasn't what I had suddenly realized. What the back of my mind was asking me was why I hadn't told her about the dreamplane.

The notion gave me a sharp twinge. In the same instance that thought occurred to me, I finally took note of how Bernstein was dressed. My brain flooded with facts, pointing out that it showed concern on her part, that she had rushed to my aid in nothing more than a towel. That after finding me unharmed she had not hurried off to make herself more presentable.

That she was not bothered by our close proximity.

It didn't take a genius to figure out that in that moment I could have, for lack of a less juvenile phrase, made my move. Considering all that had just happened, it would not really have been all that hard to play on her sympathies—present myself as vulnerable—and have an evening that would've made Shibley moan over in jealousy.

But, a different section of my mind whispered, the very reason she had acted as she had so far was that she trusted me. That she was showing concern and asking to be treated as a human being ... the same way she was treating me. It also reminded me that as the elected expert in the weird and creepy and scary crap I had an obligation to live up to my title. Deep down I had to admit that too many odd angles were beginning to come together, that if the experiences of the last few years had taught me anything, the situation I was in was screaming out to be looked at a lot more closely. Before something happened.

Before someone died.

God, I thought for a bitter second, taking one purely masculine glance at just how small Bernstein's towel was, I really do hate being a grown-up.

Then, with a sigh only I understood, I asked her;

"Marsha, have you ever heard of ... the dreamplane?"

CHAPTER EIGHT:

Our next morning's breakfast was probably a tenser affair than either Logan or Shibley had expected. Over coffee, while we waited for our orders, I told them both everything I had told Bernstein the night before. Neither one of them knew what to say... at least not at first. Finally, Shibley asked;

"So, what exactly are you telling us, Carl?"

"Got me," I admitted. "Since everyone thinks I'm the Wikipedia for crazy, that being why I was included in this little school picnic and all, I thought I should mention it."

"And this dreamplane stuff," asked Logan, "You believe all that?"

"I've been told a lot about it," I reminded him. "But last night was the first time I ever experienced it. Now, maybe I was just dreaming I was there, but like I said, the real experts on this crap say thinking like that is just kidding yourself." I took a long pull on my coffee, then added;

"Basically, the prevailing theory is, if you see red dust and purple mountains, you're there."

We batted the whole thing around throughout our meal, but in the end when our guide came into the hotel restaurant to tell us everything was ready for our departure, depart we did. First off, we had no real choice. And second, it wasn't as if I'd had a premonition of doom or anything.

Discussing the whole thing as rationally as we could, we agreed that if my meeting Smiley, along with my dream, meant anything, it most likely meant we were being warned not to disturb whatever version of the seventy-two we might find in the mountains. Since we weren't actually looking for it, since we only wanted to get into the area, get our interviews and photographs and video—and then get the hell out of Dodge—it didn't seem as if we had all that much to worry about.

By the time we were paying our bill and heading out to the front of the hotel, the four of us were in agreement—we were looking for drug warriors and a story. Nothing more. If we found a lost city with seventy-two temples filled with monks lighting candles or cleaning vegetables, we would be very careful to leave it alone and to encourage the same behavior in others. As best we could tell that was all the universe wanted from us and we were more than willing to deliver.

Our guide was a short fellow, wiry, dark skin, black hair, dark eyes. He possessed a wide smile which would have worked better as a wide grin due to fact he was missing three of his front teeth. When introductions were made, he told us to call him He'chos. If we had any problems with either of the two lackeys working under him, he made it clear we were to inform him immediately and that he would deal with them—which was fine by me.

I've been in similar situations before, and seen Americans cause themselves incredible amounts of grief for simply not going with the local flow. He'chos knew his men, knew their strengths and weaknesses. Knew how far they could be trusted or relied upon. We did not.

It's sorta like those sneaker factories everyone got into an uproar about a few years back. American companies having work done in foreign countries where they used child labor. Shocking. Horrible. Children slaving for pennies so lazy, greedy corporations could save some money. One way to look at it—granted.

The other side of that coin, however, is the fact that those greedy American corporations were paying the locals three and four times what they could make from any of their domestic companies. There was also the fact that this was work these kids could do without risking their lives, like so many of the other jobs available to them. These were countries where if every family member wasn't pulling their weight, everyone starved.

Yeah, I know it feels great to be a white knight and protect the innocent and all, but reality has to be served. Force the American companies to pay wages comparable to what they would have to pay American workers, and then the companies lose any incentive to not simply have the work done in America and save the shipping costs. That, of course, triples the cost of the sneakers, which then starts a different set of protests, and removes the money from the foreign economy making certain families by the hundreds go hungry.

I'm not saying there are any easy answers. I'm just saying that if He'chos told me he was going to punish one of his men for this or that, I for one was not about to start playing protector of the innocent. It was his job to get us into the mountains—an area filled with natural pitfalls, wild animals, poisonous insects, and murderous drug gangs—and back out again in one piece. For those that can't figure it out, this was an arrangement I was all for.

He'chos, one of his fellows, and Shibley rode in the first truck, Logan, Bernstein and I followed in the second, driven by our last native bearer. I use the old Tarzan movie terminology simply because He'chos never introduced his workers. Both of them were thin, clean shaven, quiet men with the same dark hair and skin and eyes as their boss. They were so similar they could have been twins. And, since neither of them even attempted to speak to us, we were all happy enough to dub them Abbott and Costello and leave worker/employer communications up to He'chos.

Our vehicles were in somewhat better shape than I had expected. The lead car was a black SUV that had the look of having been at one time a security vehicle for someone powerful. It was showing a bit of rust, and had more than a handful of dents. But, its windows had the thickness of bulletproof glass, and more than a few of its bruises appeared to have been caused by gunfire.

The secondary transport was more of a bus than a private vehicle. It had rowed seats, a storage area in the back where our luggage had been piled along with various supplies. It did not appear to be bulletproof in the least, but its tires were over-sized, and its stick shift had enough extra gear options to let me believe it could handle any manner of terrain we might want to throw at it.

Thanks to He'chos' no-nonsense approach to his job, our little party got under way without any delays. We'd finished breakfast at roughly 8:30AM, and by 9:00 we were out of the city and headed into the wilderness beyond. Not that we had left all signs of civilization behind, but think about it. Drive out of L.A. or New York or Chicago, and before long you're surrounded by trees. We don't think anything of it when we're home, because we know there's going to be something down the road. But, leave the country and suddenly most people begin to think they're going to see a sign reading "Abandon Hope All Ye Who Enter Here" around the next bend.   We   had been given a two-way radio so we could stay in touch with Shibley. The guides had their own set. Not long after we left the Quito city limits, Shibley contacted us, letting us know our day would be spent on the road, that we would reach the foothills of the mountains that evening in time to set up camp.

His report proved correct. After some ten hours of bouncing along, we reached a small village that had no hotel or anything one might consider an alternative. Under He'chos' direction, Abbott and Costello set up three tents—two large, one small—moved our luggage into them, and then began preparing dinner. To our surprise, one of the larger tents was for Logan and myself, the other for Shibley and He'chos, and the smaller tent in between the two larger ones for Bernstein. Our comedy team was expected to take turns keeping watch, one of them sleeping in the bus while the other kept his weather eye on things.

Dinner was hot, which was about all I remember about it. After a sweaty day of breathing the dust kicked up from a few hundred miles of twisting dirt roads, I was ready to sleep, even if it was on a cot. My worthy colleagues seemed to be of the same opinion. Breakfast was equally forgettable. The next day's drive went even slower because the terrain was growing more formidable. Our boys proved to be great drivers, losing no wheels or time getting us up into the mountains. The heat subsided somewhat, as did the dust, as we gained altitude, but that evening's sleep was almost as muggy as the night before.

The second day's drive did not last as long as the first. That was because it had been prearranged we would camp in a certain spot where we would be met sooner or later by representatives from both sides. For those who've never figured it out, the third world loves the American media. They know the power there is to be claimed by those who can get access to it, and will do everything they can to make certain our cameras can get suitable, spontaneous footage, no matter how many takes are required.

Having reached our second campsite early enough to relax a bit before dinner, I decided to do just that. The bus had, amongst its varied supplies, several antique folding chairs. Setting one up, I planted myself comfortably in the shade, determined to take a long, relaxing nap before dinner. Shutting my eyes, I did my best to doze off as quickly as possible.

I had no idea how long I had been snoring away when an unfamiliar voice came to me through the darkness. As I struggled to focus on it, the words became clearer, until finally I heard;

"Tell me, Senor Kolchak ... what do you know of the seventy-two?"

My first reaction was to sigh to myself, wondering if every dream I was going to have for the foreseeable future was going to revolve around that one particular number. Then, as I felt my arm being prodded by something hard and circular, I heard the question again. Opening my eyes, I saw that the population of our camp had increased exponentially. I also noticed that all the new members of our little community were male, and armed. Like the fellow prodding me just above the elbow with the barrel of his machine gun. As I blinked, his obvious superior asked;

"Mr. Kolchak ... I was asking you about the seventy-two."

Swallowing hard, I thought to myself, yes, you were, weren't you?

CHAPTER NINE:

"Ah, hello ..." I started off with aloud, the best version of clever I could come up with at that moment. "Ummmmm ... excuse me...?"

The fellow questioning me was tall, taller than anyone I'd seen since we gotten off the plane in Quito. Another thing that set him apart from everyone else was the fact he did not appear to be sweating. Although the heat and humidity both had trailed off a touch as we'd entered the mountains, it was still plenty hot, though you couldn't tell it looking at this guy.

"Come, Senor Kolchak ... do not waste my time. It is too valuable. And besides, I think you will find it is in your best interests to cooperate with me."

Looking around as best I could without being overly insulting to our new friend, as far as I could tell he and his companions must have simply walked up out of the trees and taken over. I could see Logan, He'chos and Costello, and they all appeared to be as helpless as I was—the three of them all holding their hands up above their heads while they stared at guns pointed in their general direction.

"First off," I said, sputtering, playing up the fact I was still half-asleep, which basically I was, "let me say that as soon as I can wake up completely, you will have my complete and utter cooperation. No problem. Guaranteed. However, I would like to warn you up front that ... I don't really know all that much about the seventy-two."

"You don't, eh?"

"No, sir," I answered, trying to make certain my tone reflected the fact I was determined to stay alive until dinner, and if possible, maybe even after that. "To be perfectly honest, up until four days ago, I'd never even heard of them."

"And what have you heard during the last four days, Senor Kolchak?"

Blinking hard, trying to drive the sleep from my eyes, I realized my questioner had been calling me by name. What can I tell you—sometimes it takes a moment. Feeling a dry tickle in my throat, I tried swallowing to make it go away, but that started me coughing. Putting up my hand, palm outward, signaling that I just needed a minute and that I would appreciate not getting shot, I managed to get myself back under control quick enough to keep any of the newcomers from getting overly irritated. Deciding to take a chance, I asked;

"Excuse me, but since you seem to know who I am, might I ask to whom I have the pleasure of speaking?"

"I am Nestor Rhiheto."

"Thank you. And, ah ... Mr. Rhiheto, it just dawned on me that I'm sitting while you're standing. I don't want to make any sudden movements with

Machine Gun Kelly here, but if I'm showing the kind of disrespect that's going to get me in dutch—"

Rhiheto waved a hand pleasantly to cut me off.

"It is not to worry," he assured me. "I am not stepped out of some sort of movie. I chose to stand, am more comfortable doing so. I also had your sleep disturbed. You were already sitting. I have no problem being reasonable. And, all I am reasonably expecting from you is that you answer my question. Tell me, Senor Kolchak, what do you know of the seventy-two?"

"I know they must be." When Rhiheto merely stared at me, I said;

"That's really all I know."

After which I told him everything. I told him about Smile for the Golden Morning and his candles, about my grocers and their vegetables—everything. Little as that everything was I gave it up without a second thought. And, why not? There were no lives at stake. I wasn't revealing state secrets. A man with a gun demands details about your dreams, especially the ones which don't make a lick of sense to you; I say "tell him." When I finished, I apologized, saying;

"I'm sorry, but that really is all I have."

While Rhiheto considered what I'd told him, I took the moment to begin to panic. I still hadn't seen or heard any trace of Shibley or Bernstein, or Abbott, for that matter. I'd been able to count a minimum of fourteen new faces, each of them attached to well-armed bodies. Hoping to forestall the use of any of

63

those arms, I asked;

"Mr. Rhiheto, if you don't mind me asking, are you one of the gentlemen we came here to meet?"

"Yes, Senor Kolchak," he admitted without hesitation, "I am. Since it is not my intention to frighten anyone, I shall explain to you what has happened." I swallowed again, hoping the story I was about to hear had a happy ending.

"I am the head of what has been labeled on the television as 'the Mountain Family.' Our main rivals, the other side in the current shooting war, that is Hector Lenzano's organization." I nodded absently, having been told in L.A. that those were the groups we would be contacting.

"As I believe you must be aware, the cocaine business is a very profitable one. The Lenzanos and my own family, we are both ... very rich. More money than anyone could ever need. Money enough to buy us whatever we desire."

"Well, I envy you that, sir."

Rhiheto smiled, admiring my honesty. What the hell, I thought. Why try and kid him? After all, who didn't want to be that kind of rich? Risking erasing his smile, I mentally crossed my fingers, then asked;

"But it makes me a little curious. If both sides are already as wealthy as they could possibly want, then what's the fighting all about? Not trying to be rude, you understand. We were sent down here to find these kinds of things out. You could just think of this as part of the interview. I mean, a lot of people have died. If not for money, then what?"

"You see," the drug lord said in a loud voice to all his men, "this is a man who knows how to do his job." Focusing his attention on me, he then said;

"If I had a dozen men like you in my employ ..."

He then waved his left hand absently in the air before him, as if to indicate he had no words for all he could accomplish with twelve men who knew how to do their jobs. At the same time, one of his soldiers came forward with one of the other folding chairs from our bus. Setting it up for his leader, he then turned and left without a word as Rhiheto settled into the seat. As he turned to face me, he dismissed the guard that had been standing over me, announcing he was confident I was not going to do anything foolish. I wanted to say that there were plenty of people who might argue I was always capable of doing something foolish, but I knew Machine Gun Kelly or one of his pals could be summoned fairly easily, so I decided to simply keep my big yap shut. Rhiheto filled the silence created by my reticence.

"Senor Kolchak, I am a fairly good judge of character. You do not impress me as a stupid man. I believe you have told me all you know. You might not think it could be of any use to anyone, but you have indeed told me quite a lot. Because of that, I will tell you what you wish to know."

For a moment I relaxed. We had traveled south to discover what the current drug war was all about, and what it might mean to the safety of the rumored city of the seventy-two. After less than two days we were about to get one side of the story handed to us. Reaching into the bag at my side—slowly, carefully—I asked if there was any objection to my recording our conversation. Rhiheto magnanimously told me to proceed.

"The Lenzanos, they are not fighting us for, what would you call it ... 'market shares' of the cocaine industry. As I said, both our sides have all the money we need, all the business we can handle. What we are looking for, is the seventy-two. The battles we have had, these have occurred when our forces have come across one another as we search the mountains for them."

"But," I interrupted, forgetting myself, "why? What are they? I mean, if you already have everything you could want, what could they possibly offer you?"

"The stories are as old as the languages in which they are told. Somewhere in these mountains, lies the lost city of the seventy-two. Within it, dwells power enough for any man to rule the cosmos. We are, both sides, in a race to find it before the other does so."

"But ..." I answered, more than a little perplexed, "there are all sorts of rumors in the world. You said these things you'd heard were just stories. Why are you suddenly taking them so seriously—killing one another over them? I don't get it."

"This is understandable, Senor Kolchak. As you said before, when the monk told you of the seventy-two, it made no impression on you. It was nothing

66

more than a foolish story in a world of such tales. But, after your dream, you began to feel a pattern coming together. One you could not ignore. Am I correct?" After I agreed that he was, Rhiheto went on, saying;

"It is the same for us. There are many legends which run through these mountains. A man could spend ten lifetimes trying to track them all down without ever finding a single piece of evidence to back up any one of them."

I was about to ask another pointless question, when suddenly my mind jumped ahead. Needing to know the answer to the notion which had just formed in my brain, I asked;

"But ... you found something, didn't you? Something that proves the seventy-two is real—yes?"

Rhiheto merely nodded. As my genuine excitement continued to mount, I asked the drug king what exactly had been discovered. Smiling wide, he told me;

"We have one of them."

"One of ..."

I almost asked another useless question, but caught myself just in time. Nodding to me again, Rhiheto told me;

"Yes—we have one of the seventy-two."

CHAPTER TEN:

I have to admit, there's a side to my profession which does not show off those of us who practice it in the best light. As Rhiheto revealed that he had gotten a hold of some person or another that was a member of this mysterious seventy-two, my first thoughts were not for that person's safety. I didn't wonder if it was a man or woman—it never occurred to me for even an instant that it might be a child. I didn't consider that drug lords searching the jungle for short cuts to power might turn to torture to get the information they wanted.

No, all I considered was "the story." Suddenly there was a lead, a link to credibility. A reason to be interested. A possibility for a by-line. It's like that moment in the first Raiders movie, when Indiana Jones has the drop on the bad guys and threatens to blow up the Ark. The bad guy bluffs him, tells him to go ahead and do it because he knows Jones won't—because he knows Jones has to know the truth. It's the kind of thing that keeps a cameraman filming a disaster instead of running out to help someone.

I could see the approval of my reaction in Rhiheto's face. He knew I was intrigued. Smiling, he asked;

"So, you really didn't know the seventy-two referred to seventy-two people, did you?"

"Like I told you, candles, dreams ... I figured it was just another legend. The world is full of them, you know."

"This is true, senor ... but I must admit, a man such as yourself, I thought you would have more interest in ... how can I say ... something like this."

"A man such as myself...?"

And then it hit me. Granted, I had only been awake a couple of minutes, but it came back to me ... the fact that this guy in the middle of nowhere knew my name. As I blinked hard, finally driving the last of the sleep from my eyes, I saw Shibley and Bernstein being herded across the campsite to where Logan and the others were being held. Bernstein looked as worried as any of the others, but there was something in Shibley's manner that told me once again I might not be holding all the cards I needed to win the next hand. Before Rhiheto could respond, I said;

"You know who I am."

"I do."

Turning my head, I stared at Shibley—glared, really—until I saw in his eyes that he realized what it was I had just figured out. The tiniest trace of a smile curled the edges of his mouth as he raised his eyebrows several times, indicating that he knew what I was thinking. Turning back to Rhiheto, I asked;

"I guess my big question is, did you know who I was before or after the American State Department got in touch with you?"

"Truly excellent," answered the drug lord, his head bobbing up and down in appreciation. "You are everything I was told you would be. But, before I wander and you suspect I am trying to change the subject, the answer to your question is 'before.' I had indeed heard of you 'before.' Why else would I have asked for you?"

The rest of the story got spread out on the table fairly quickly after that. Seems State hadn't contacted Shibley first. In its usual effort to keep the peace from behind the scenes, it had contacted both Rhiheto and the Lenzano family, to see if they might be able to work something out quietly. To the bright boys and girls at State, the idea that people in the twenty-first century could be killing one another in an attempt to be the first to find a lost city was insanity. That the combatants expected to find some sort of weapon in this parcel of misplaced real estate that could turn them into world conquerors on a planet bristling with nuclear weapons had apparently left the thin tie set at State speechless.

Thus, believing they were dealing with essentially heavily-armed children, the government types had asked what could stop the fighting. The Lenzanos, being a younger, upstart bunch, had spit firmly in the general direction of Washington, D.C., refusing to deal with them. Somehow they got it into their head that the government of the United States was no more trustworthy than their own, and opted out of the negotiations. That left Rhiheto.

"I told them, help me find the lost city of the seventy-two, and there would be no more violence. They photographed this whole area from outer space, x-rays, heat searchers, some things I can't really claim to understand ... and all of it led to ... nothing. They could find ... nothing. So, I told them ... you want to prove this good faith of yours to me, get me Carl Kolchak."

I grimaced, more internally than anything else, not seeing the profit in insulting all the new guests we had in camp. How, I wondered, do I have the luck I do? What mood was God in when he decided that this was the life I got?

"It's true, Carl," Shibley called out. "When State came to me, they made it clear Senor Rhiheto would only play ball if you were sent down for him to work with."

Shibley's words struck me hard—harder than I would have imagined. I hadn't needed to strike it lucky, didn't have to track down poor, stupid Denny Bott—I would have been on the team no matter what. I wanted to get up and walk over to Shibley and brain him. I wanted to scream, to throw a fit—to just boil over about having been used yet again by people who apparently thought I should be running over with gratitude for being sent into the jungle to face the guns of deluded drug killers.

I didn't do any of that, however. I learned to control my temper back in the sandbox, at least during those times when not doing so could likely get one's clock cleaned—free of charge. Instead, I shoved aside all that which I couldn't do anything about, and asked instead;

"So, you get the Internet down here, do ya? And you waste it reading about ... me?"

Rhiheto smiled, assuring me that I was his first choice, if not his only choice to help him find the city. When I asked him why, he told me;

"Senor Kolchak, you have written about seeing, and battling on occasion, and more often that not running away from, all manner of strange and unusual things. You claim to have seen ghosts, vampires, werewolves, zombies, creatures from other worlds even ... is this not true?" When I agreed it was, the drug lord continued, asking me;

"All of these things of which you wrote ... tell me, sir ... do you believe them? Did you actually battle a swamp creature, a thing made out of electricity ... witches ... all of it, I ask you now, when you wrote of these things, were you telling the truth?"

Nodding my head sadly, like a child admitting to having stolen candy from their baby brother, I answered;

"Yes ... as best I understood whatever was going on at the time, yes—I stand behind it all."

I looked around again, wondering just what I was opening the door to by saying such. By this time it was clear Rhiheto had come into the area with at least thirty men. They had swept in from all angles, making certain they gathered up our entire crew. They weren't threatening anyone overtly, but everyone in our party had been herded together and were being held while I had my little chat. Clapping his hands together, Rhiheto answered my questions for me by explaining what was to happen next.

"Very well, you believe. I believe. Then it is time for you to do what you came here to do."

"How so, if you don't mind me asking?"

"Quite simple. You came to report on two warring drug cartels, battling each other over an ancient legend. You came to get interviews and photos and video and, if possible, to prove or disprove the existence of the seventy-two—correct?" When I agreed with his statement, Rhiheto said;

"Then that is what will be done. Tonight, I will answer whatever questions any and all of you may have. Tomorrow, two of you will go with your hired men to do the same with the Lenzanos." The drug lord paused for effect, then smiled as he said;

"And while they do that, you and I, and a few dozen of my close friends here, we shall press onward into the mountains. And, under the direction of you, senor, we shall find the seventy-two.
And then all their vast and ancient secrets shall be mine."

CHAPTER ELEVEN:

That evening passed all too quickly. We four gringos were treated like honored guests, but the feeling of it was much the kind of "honor" turkeys must feel come November. I'm not saying there were hints of treachery ahead, that I felt I was being lied to about anything. It was far more along the lines of just how comfortable were we supposed to feel around a major player in the world-wide illegal drug trade and his most trusted mercenaries.

It had to be admitted that Rhiheto certainly kept his word about accessibility. After dinner, he held court, answering any questions we had for him, not only allowing audio recording, but video as well. Logan and Bernstein both had considerable backgrounds in "presentational journalism," and got several hours of footage from different angles, assuring our bosses would be quite pleased with our efforts.

The drug lord had no problem revealing how many millions a day he made from "his beloved North American clientele," how many rooms there were in his mansion, how large his swimming pool was, how many judges, district attorneys, mayors, police chiefs and the such, he employed to keep his operations running smoothly, et cetera.

His emotions ran a little higher when we began

discussing his competitors. Rhiheto considered himself a commercial entrepreneur and a gentleman. The Lenzano clan, however, in his opinion were thugs and opportunists. Where he supplied product, they were blood-letting murderers. In a way, he almost had a point. Several years back, Rhiheto had been the biggest player in the marketplace, surrounded by dozens of smaller suppliers. Although the cocaine business has never been as amiable as say, the rivalry between fast food outlets, there had been a certain harmony between those doing their best to fulfill the needs of a self-destructive public.

That had changed when the Lenzano family joined the game. They had started by buying out the business of several of the small fry, and then driving the others out of the field one by one. Murder… political payoffs, destruction of poppy fields, slaughtering work villages—whatever it took to destroy the competition. Now, they had but one competitor left— our host.

Sure, Rhiheto wasn't quite as clean as he made himself sound, and the Lenzanos weren't quite as bad, but for once vested self-interest wasn't actually that far from the truth.

The next morning, Shibley and Logan found they would get their chance to prove that assertion. They were picked by Rhiheto to leave with He'chos, Abbott and Costello to get the loyal opposition's side of the case. Logan and Bernstein had to be split simply because they were the camera jockeys—one of them had to be with each team. His choice of Bernstein over Logan only helped solidify his alpha maleness. I, of course, was Rhiheto's prize, and that, as they say, was that.

The rented vehicles left with Shibley and Logan. Our new host had plenty of his own. Two of them took point, Bernstein choosing to ride in the lead vehicle so she might get some scenic footage to cut in with the rest. I rode with Rhiheto in the third, followed by two additional carriers. All his vehicles were of local origin, large, heavy, armored four-wheelers built for survival. Even our host's personal cruiser had few amenities the others did not.

As we started out for the mountains, Rhiheto made himself a drink—one of those few amenities I mentioned before—offering me one as well. I accepted, just to be sociable, of course. After we'd both had a few sips, he asked what was bothering me. Weighing my options, I decided that since my host was no idiot, there was no point in insulting him with a lie.

"Well," I said, praying in the back of my head that I wasn't as stupid as everyone seems to think I am, "I don't want to appear rude or anything, but I was wondering ... why would you let Shibley and Logan go to the Lenzanos?"

"A good question, a fair concern." Our host took another sip from his drink, then stared into my eyes, telling me;

"I want your cooperation, Senor Kolchak, so first

off, harming your companions in front of you would gain me nothing. This only means that perhaps I simply left others behind to eliminate them after we were gone. But again, this would help nothing. You see, I want them to reach the Lenzanos."

Our conversation was interrupted by a jarring bump as we hit some sort of obstacle which shook the carrier roughly enough to almost knock my hat from my head. I ended up with alcohol down my hand, but Rhiheto, apparently accustomed to such distractions, didn't seem to lose a drop. Smiling sympathetically at me, he continued, saying;

"First off, what could they tell them, that I am searching for the seventy-two? They know this. They are well aware. However, your friends' arrival, finding them, this will slow them down. Your State Department only contacted me. The Lenzanos will want to find out everything they can. This will take time. They will also want to use this wonderful opportunity to influence the American public much as I did. This will also take time."

"So," I said, taking a sip from what alcohol I had still within my tumbler, "you don't think anything will happen to them?"

"To be as honest with you as you have with me, I have no idea, actually. No businessman ever wants to kill an American. There is simply no profit to it. But, you came here looking to speak with both sides. As for my side, I have been open with you, answered all your questions, and have provided your team with detailed instructions on how to find the other side. If the Lenzanos do not behave in a like manner, what can I tell you?"

Rhiheto spread his hands wide before him, shrugging as he did so, indicating that there was little more he could do. There wasn't much I could say about it. He was right. We had come down, chasing a story, looking for rewards—knowing the risks. Granted, I'd been played for a sucker, but then, I reminded myself, what was actually new about that? Maybe the fact that for once it seemed to have worked in my favor, but there was a funny thing about that word "seemed."

What, I wondered once more, did Rhiheto actually think I could do for him? He appeared to know more about the seventy-two, and had known it longer, than I did. I had no idea what they were, had never heard of their lost city, did not have the faintest idea what might be inside it, et cetera. As far as I could tell, I was useless to him. A clever fellow, he could see that I obviously had more on my mind than the eventual fate of my comrades. Waving his free hand in the air gently in a dismissive manner, he told me;

"You worry so much, Senor Kolchak. Please, let me assure you, I do not expect anything from you that you shall not be able to provide."

"More than willing to believe you," I assured him, meaning it, "but I think my problem stems from not actually having even the slightest idea as to *what* it is you believe I'll be able to provide."

Rhiheto slid his tumbler into a cupholder built

78

into the wall of our vehicle, apparently unable to communicate effectively with only one free hand. He reminded me of Vincenzo in that way. Fully articulate once he had two hands, he said;

"More than one person commenting about you on the Internet has said you are ... eh, like a magnet for the beyond. I need such a thing right now." The drug lord turned slightly so he could see out the side window. Staring into the passing jungle, he said;

"This war, to find the seventy-two ... it is destroying both sides. Hundreds have died. Good men, many. I understand that you know no more of them than you have told. And, the one member of the seventy-two we have captured ... he will not talk." Not wanting to know the answer to a question, but needed to, I asked;

"How hard did you try to make him talk?"

"He was not tortured. I assume that is what you mean. It's not a wise thing. Not in this case." I must have raised an eyebrow or given some sort of signal indicating I had my doubts, for my host smiled at me, saying;

"I understand. Have I had answers beaten from people ... of course. Such is merely business. But not this, this is something more than mere commerce. You do not injure one who may be blessed by gods, or ... protected by demons."

"Demons?"

I admit I said the word with a curious fear. Of all the terrors and creepies and just plain bizarre-O nut stuff I've come across, very little of it has actually tracked to matters of faith. I've seen enough to make me believe in a Heaven and a Hell, and don't relish the idea of coming across additional proof. More than a little concerned, I asked;

"Senor Rhiheto, please ... just so I don't die of a heart attack before I finish my drink, what little I haven't spilled all over myself ... demons? What are we getting into? What is it you expect to find? And how, again ... please ... do you think I can help?"

"Quite simply, my friend," said the drug lord as he reached out and clasped my knee, "I don't know. There are stories that say the lost city of the seventy-two is filled with incomparable riches, others that it holds magical weapons, maybe both. Maybe there is nothing."

Releasing his hold then, Rhiheto reached for his tumbler. Taking a sip, he then spread his hands wide, laughing as he said;

"Who knows? To me, this is a challenge. When a man gathers to himself great wealth and power, he begins to lose interest in the material world. After all, how many rare paintings can you own, women can you bed, cars can you drive ... money—how quickly it becomes worthless."

Having never had that much of it, I decided to simply take his word on the matter.

"I do this ... because I *want* to. Because I want to *know* the truth. If I become a god, wonderful. If I am cast into the fires, so be it. Life needs fire. Men need

adventure, Senor Kolchak. This ... this will be mine."
The drug lord took another sip from his tumbler,
paused, took another, and then told me;

"As for you, I wish to put you together with our
other guest. If you are a magnet, the kind of magnet
I need, then perhaps the way will be revealed at last.
If not, I will send you home, you and the camera-
woman. But, if we do learn something, then into the
mountains we will go. And you will record the story of
what happens, and you will tell the world."

I listened politely, nodding from time to time, and
keeping my big yap shut. I had left L.A., thinking I
knew what kind of danger I was heading into. I had-
n't cared about dying. Not if it meant a chance at a
story that would put my by-line in front of the entire
world. The kind of death I worry about is the kind I
was headed for back in Hollywood—death by bore-
dom, by neglect, or considering how much I was paid,
maybe even by starvation.

But this was different. Rhiheto was a type I'd met
before, curious, intrigued, but without knowledge.
Guys who flock to zombie movies, girls that get all hot
and bothered over the idea of vampires, these morons
are so hopelessly stupid it's a wonder they can dress
themselves. I've come across vampires and zombies
both, watched them tear human beings apart as if they
were nothing.

And, do understand, it's not the physical ease
with which they do these things that frightens me, it's
the mental ease. The fact that they can kill without a

second thought is what makes them so truly horrifying. Denny Bott, the serial killer I "brought to justice," was just a frightened little man who wanted to be caught. But that's because he was still human.

Rhiheto was a man who had ordered murders, most likely committed some. He was, almost certainly, despite his cultured accent and polished manners, as coldblooded a monster as I had ever met. And he wanted me to help him penetrate some sort of veil of darkness which had kept something hidden from mankind since the beginning of time. Something, as they use to say, man was not supposed to know about.

Laughing, I nodded to my host, tipped my tumbler in his direction, and then drained every last drop from it, hoping that as soon as I was finished he'd offer to refill it.

CHAPTER TWELVE:

Ants.

For some reason, they were all I could see. Ants everywhere. Their alien heads, their terrible faces, big and menacing, overwhelming my field of vision no matter which way I turned my head. All I could hear were their mandibles snapping before me, slicing the air, the dull buzz of their antennae twitching, vibrating,… slashing back and forth.

Ants—there was no other way to say it, there was just nothing but ants. Millions of them, crawling across everything, marching in rows. The unescapable sound of their rhythmically trampling feet echoing rang through the jungle—drowning out all other sound. Sending everything that could move fleeing before them.

The tens of millions of them were everywhere, crawling across everything. They were not biting or stinging. Not carrying anything. Not doing anything at all but marching—relentlessly… feverishly.

In rows.

Long columns, moving toward some forward position I could not see, could not imagine. Insanely long lines of them, marching across the face of the world, blotting the sky. Everywhere.

Everywhere.

There were red ones. And black ones. Some were the tiniest insects I had ever seen anywhere. Some were so large the thought of them filled me with city dweller dread at the thought of having to live with such things—three and four inches in length. I felt myself shudder as I watched all of them following one another. All of them marching—marching.

In their unyielding rows.

And that was when it hit me. Once again, I was dreaming. I had to be. I didn't think I'd stumbled onto the dreamplane once more. I had no recollection of scarlet fields or purple mountains filled with lightning, and that I'd been assured repeatedly by those who knew such things had to be the case. Therefore, I told myself I with a touch of relief, I was simply dreaming once more.

Never one to leave a good thing alone, however, I couldn't resist asking myself, exactly when was it I had fallen asleep?

And, why in the world was I dreaming of ants?

Whatever reason had fixated my mind on ants, I could not stop envisioning them. No matter how hard I tried to take control of my dream—which all of us have been able to manage from time to time—I could banish the intruders massing across the inside of my brain.

They were everywhere. On everything. When I looked down they covered the ground. When I looked up they were crawling across the sky. They were the landscape, the horizon—they were all of reality and I couldn't do anything to stop it.

Closing my dreaming eyes to the sight of them, I did my best to ignore the never-ending rows. Pulling my brain away from simply wondering why I was seeing nothing but ants, I forced it to begin thinking of them as an answer to some question I had to be attempting to formulate.

What, I tried to reason, did the ants represent? Good or bad? Were they a warning or a blessing? Why ants? What were ants that nothing else was? Why not birds or cows or jellyfish? Why, I asked myself again, poking myself a little harder,... was I dreaming of ants? What was I trying to tell myself? What in the name of heaven could be so all important about ants?

Then, as I questioned myself in the darkness, suddenly a terrible dread fell over me. Ants marched in groups, in straight lines when they were going somewhere...somewhere important. To a place they were going to conquer, or ravage. Ants, I remembered, were the only species on the planet besides man that made war, that committed genocide, that created slaves.

But, even as I questioned where the ants were headed, why they were headed there, I began to feel something—a sensation. An irritation. One created by the ants. After having swarmed across everything else, they had begun to crawl on me. Across my feet, over my ankles, up my legs, knees, thighs, hips—

Tiny legs scurrying, covering me, two and three

rows thick, crawling over each other, a million of them—swarming over my skin, under my clothing—a hundred million of them, running across the top of my clothes, a hundred thousand tread marks on my penis, clambering over my abdomen, up my chest, across my shoulders, down my arms, up my neck, more and more, faster and faster, forearms, chin, elbows, ears, on my wrists on my eyes in my hair my fingers my mouth—

I screamed.

I screamed in my dream and in the real world, loud enough to wake myself, and draw attention. Easy to do when you're falling over, rolling off of something, striking the ground, rolling across it, trying to crush ants, still screaming—

"Senor Kolchak—"

Somehow I managed to recognize my name, enough of a wake-up call for me to remember that I had been dreaming, to notice there were no ants crawling across me. Not in my mouth or on my eyes or anywhere near me. Blinking harshly, I turned my head from side to side, trying to remember where I was, what I had been doing, making certain I was really away from the ants.

"Senor, I believe you were dreaming."

I looked up, focusing on the speaker. It was Rhiheto. Suddenly, memory began to flood my consciousness. As my startled condition began to fade, I noticed I was still frantically brushing myself off, swatting at the bugs which had existed only in my dream.

Feeling a trifle stupider than normal, I finally grabbed hold of myself, answering;

"Yeah, umm ... that would be the size of it."

"And what, if I might ask, were you dreaming about?"

"Ants," I told the drug lord, immediately wondering if I should have said anything. In my still half-groggy state, the voices I tend to dismiss were able to shout with a bit more volume within my mind. One after another they reminded me that Rhiheto was up to no good. That he was looking for a sacred place, one it was almost guaranteed he should not find.

Still, I reasoned with myself, all I told him was that I was dreaming of ants. How was that going to cause anyone any problems? Handing harmless information over to killers with their own armies has always simply seemed like common sense to me. Dismissing my fears as simply more paranoia than even I needed to lug around, I shook my head while taking a couple of deep breaths, working at pulling myself together when I noticed something.

As my memories solidified, everything from before I went to sleep came rushing back to me. We had reached the base camp for that evening. More of Rhiheto's men and equipment had bee waiting for us there. So was the drug lord's prisoner. He turned out to be a small man, dressed in little more than a loin cloth. He was a short, brown-skinned fellow, obviously a local. His weathered skin and hair bespoke an outdoor lifestyle.

Remembering him made me look around a bit more, and finally everything came together for me. I had come awake in a large tent, one big enough for Rhiheto to stand comfortably erect. Large enough for him to stand in the middle and not crowd me or the cot I had been sleeping on before I'd knocked it over while falling to the floor. Large enough to store a number of crates and duffles, and another cot—atop of which lay their prisoner. Bound and gagged. Brought in to sleep next to me, to see if Rhiheto's theory of me being some kind of magnet for the weird was true.

The drug lord had seemed pleased when I'd mentioned ants, and at that moment I knew why. I had seen millions of ants in my dream. So many that at one point I'd thought there were a hundred million of them. There weren't a hundred million of them.

Just seventy-two million.

Finally making it to my feet, I stumbled out of the tent and began eyeing the ground. Rhiheto was already outside, doing the same thing. We both saw what we were looking for at the same time.

Ants.

Marching. In straight lines. Thousands—hundreds of thousands ... millions of them.

They were, for the most part, small and insignificant, and so much a part of the jungle scenery that if you weren't actually looking for them, you would never see them. But they were there. Millions of them. Marching along.

Leading the way to the seventy-two and their lost city.

Before me my host was shouting in Spanish. All around the camp men were jumping to obey his orders. Behind me, Rhiheto's native prisoner was sobbing softly on his cot.

If I'd had any sense I would have joined him.

CHAPTER THIRTEEN:

"Look at them, Senor Kolchak."

Rhiheto's hand swept over the jungle floor before us. Ants of all types were pouring forward across the landscape in a staggering series of straight lines. Cutting through the jungle, they looked as if they were sweeping up from the lowlands and heading on into the highest part of the mountains before us.

"A moment ago, they were not to be noticed," said the drug lord. "But now, now your eye can not leave them—can it?"

He was right. It was practically beyond belief that they could have been streaming by us earlier like this and no one had noticed them. But then it hit me, maybe we hadn't. Maybe none of us had noticed them earlier because maybe they hadn't actually *been* there earlier. Maybe they only began moving because I'd been sleeping next to one of the seventy-two. Maybe my presence only was enough to start something like this.

Rhiheto was not the first person to suggest this kind of thing to me.

"I told you, Senor Kolchak," the drug lord offered, grinning as he moved his head back and forth, first staring at me, then the ants, then me again. "I knew you would be all that we would need to win through."

For a second the almost serene look on Rhiheto's face remained, the happiness of it making him appear almost innocent. It didn't stay that way for long. The grin flowed into a smirk, then a sneer. I could see the tiny gears turning in the back of his mind, whirling away as he imagined his way through the next couple of days. Breaking into this lost city of the seventy-two, looting it, gathering up its riches or weapons or whatever it was that had to be protected, using the new-found wealth or power to crush his enemies—

The simplicity of it played out across his face so clearly it was frightening.

He only spent a moment lost in his reverie, however, and then the drug lord was back to business. With a snap of his fingers, Rhiheto called forth two of his men, snapping off orders to them in Spanish. As he turned to several others, the first two began relaying orders to some of the others. As I watched the activity unfold, I began to realize that most of the camp had already been struck and packed away. My host must have assumed something was going to come from my little nap, and had decided to be ready to follow my dreams wherever they might lead. That was something else I found frightening.

I hadn't really had a chance to think through any of what had happened to me since I'd arrived in Ecuador. Everything had been moving too quickly. It had been bad enough discovering that instead of getting a plum assignment through any means I could feel good about, I'd only been brought along because of the old Kolchak Curse. Then it had been made clear to me that for all intents and purposes, the entire assignment had been a sham—and that the curse of being me was dragging me headlong into disaster once more.

Smile for the Golden Morning had been trying to warn me that trouble was coming. Of course, why he had to do his whole mystic hoodoo number on me I couldn't tell you. Sure, I let my greed and my fragile ego get me tangled up in the whole mess, but I was also thinking that it wasn't all my fault. I was thinking then if he had just said, "Hey, Kolchak, don't go to South America or you're going to end up dead," that most likely I would have paid him more attention.

It _is_ possible.

If I was half the supernatural expert everyone was beginning to think I was, I would have pegged Smiley for what he was, or at least what he represented, and that I would have paid more attention. Especially to the dreams. Hell, maybe I'd have figured out what they meant. Although, maybe not. The possibility of that was looking less and less likely, because even as Rhiheto was getting the last of the camp squared away, I had to admit that I still didn't really know what the seventy-two was. But, it did seem fairly certain I was going to find out before too long.

As the last of the drug lord's traveling circus got stored on his trucks, Marsha finally surfaced. Having finally woken up completely, I had just started to wonder where she was when she strolled into view. Apparently from the smiles on the faces of the drug thugs walking with her, and the fact she had her camera with her, she had been getting some footage of them, filling their heads with dreams of seeing themselves on television—perhaps some sort of "before they became masters of the world" kind of segment.

As Marsha drew closer, that tiny thought of mine which I'd only meant to be sarcastic began to nag at me. There was no denying the truth of it. Rhiheto, the Lenzanos, all of their men, that was why they were doing what they were doing. At the very least they expected to come down out of the mountains with chests of gold and pearls, wearing ruby crowns and diamond rings. That possibility alone was enough to guarantee bloodshed for any we found in our path.

But, the back of my mind asked me, what if the other end of the legends is true? What if there was some sort of weapon there to be found by the yahoos with whom I was camping? Some book of spells or trunk of magic powder or some other sort of mystical crap that might just give these jokers the power of the gods, or the Devil, or something?

I have to admit it was a hideous thought, one terrible enough to make my blood run cold. Despite the sweltering temperature there in the jungle, I felt my whole system chill over, felt my blood icing. After all, I couldn't just ignore the possibility that Rhiheto was right. I'd been able to laugh off a few of the notions that had been presented to me when all this nonsense had started for me, after Vegas, after every time I turned around and something else came bumping its way through the night at me.

But it was only on occasion that I could laugh with any reasonable chance of being right. For the most part, all of it had turned out to be real. Werewolves, witches, hell hounds, aliens, evil microbes, big, small, old, new, it had all been real, and it all just kept coming. No matter what part of the country I was in, what city, what kind of people, it didn't matter. It never stopped. It just kept coming. Everywhere I turned, everywhere I went, every thing I did ...

Maybe, I thought for a moment, giving the notion some credence, the Rhiheto's were right. Maybe I really was a magnet for such things. I didn't know how it could be possible, how it could have happened to me. It wasn't like I'd ever tried to find such things. I didn't go rambling through haunted houses when I was a kid, didn't tease old gypsy women who might have cursed me, didn't sleep in cemeteries on a dare.

It just wasn't fair, I told myself. I mean, it wasn't even as if I could do something about most of it. Even if I wanted to see myself as an instrument of Fate, or a tool through which the Lord was working some of His mysterious ways, or any of that nonsense, it wasn't like I was going to be able to stop Rhiheto and his private army from doing anything he wanted to the rest of the seventy-one when he got ...

And then it hit me.

Where was my bunkmate? Having no further use

for the captured native, what had the drug lord done with him? Had he simply had his men kill him? I hadn't heard any shots, but there were plenty of ways to kill people that didn't involve loud noises. I hated the fact that some part of my brain was thinking it would be my fault if the guy was dead. How, I asked myself in a panic, could it be my fault? I wasn't some superhero. I wasn't a cop or a hired gun. I never in my life accepted any kind of responsibility toward the public at large other than to attempt to keep them informed—something that, so far, the public for the most part had either jeered over or ignored.

It, I told myself again, believing myself, just wasn't fair.

Ignoring the approaching Marsha, I suddenly turned and began to cut across the clearing toward Rhiheto. I don't know what I planned on actually doing, but a part of me wanted me to do something besides simply stand around for once. Halfway to the drug lord's side, however, I spotted number seventy-two. He was still tied up, but sitting on the ground now, his back to a tree. As I slowed considerably, Rhiheto took note of me, saw me staring at the native, then said in a chuckling voice;

"Senor Kolchak, tell the truth ... you thought I had him killed, didn't you?"

"How much trouble does a 'yes' answer get me in?"

The drug lord laughed again. Apparently my humor is more entertaining in the hinterlands than on the big city circuit. Shaking his head sadly, Rhiheto walked toward me. As he drew alongside me, he admitted;

"I will tell you honestly, actually, I forgot all about our friend here. Now that you have reminded me, though, I leave it to you. What should be done with him?"

"Well," I drawled, stalling for time, trying to think my answer through and not just blurt out the first stupid thing that came into my head, unlike the way I've answered most of the other important questions posed to me over the years, "since you have the ants to follow, and ... since maybe doing him any harm might disrupt whatever, um, forces set the ants to marching in the first place ... maybe you could just let him go?"

"Why not?"

When I simply stared, most likely giving Rhiheto a fairly goofy look of puzzlement to take in, he told me;

"As you say, he has served his purpose. The ants are marching. It is all that I wanted." The drug lord, paused, then asked;

"Have I spilled blood in my time? Of course. To lie about such would be to insult you. But have I ever had anyone killed who did not deserve it? Never.! This man may have helped us unwillingly, but he did help us. That is all that matters."

With a gesture, Rhiheto indicated my bunkmate should be released. Patting me on the arm, the drug lord then pointed in the direction we should begin walking. As I watched one of his men cut the native's bonds and then even help him to his feet, Rhiheto added;

"We know where we are going, and we are going there in trucks. Our friend there is on foot. He is tired, hasn't eaten. His legs and arms are sore from being tied. He can not warn anyone of our coming. He is harmless. And the harmless do not deserve violence."

Just then Marsha caught up to us. Her camera slung over her shoulder, she made an aggressive kind of hop to announce her presence, asking in a delighted kind of girly voice;

"What'cha talking about?"

"The fact that the harmless do not deserve violence."

"Okay," she answered, looking at me as if I were the school geek who simply couldn't find a clue if he tripped over one, "there's a mood killer."

"You see," said Rhiheto, "even our lovely senorita understands. We are headed into adventure. Somewhere in the mountains ahead of us, somewhere in only a handful of miles, miracle awaits us."

I nodded in weak agreement as the three of us clambered into the second vehicle, remembering that the destruction of Sodom and Gomorrah was a miracle, too.

CHAPTER FOURTEEN:

The speed with which we could proceed was slowed considerably by the roughness of the terrain. The local roads dropped in quality dramatically as we gained altitude, finally dwindling down to paths which, as one might imagine, were not created with anything other than foot traffic in mind. Which meant, of course, that we all got out and started marching. The Kolchak Curse was running true to form.

There was no problem deciding which way to go, of course. The ants had not deserted us. They continued to lead the way, although it seemed that having captured our attention, their numbers had dropped off drastically. The millions which had marched past us back at the camp in the lowlands had thinned to mere thousands. It was enough.

I had to give Rhiheto's men credit, they could certainly move efficiently. They didn't chat, didn't allow themselves to be distracted by anything around us. Every one of them had a pack or two slung over their backs, and were carrying at least one load by hand. The drug lord had assigned a pair of them to lug Marsha and my luggage as well as their own. Lucky for me. Ms. Bernstein might have been able to keep up with our jolly band of hikers, but I'll admit it was all I could do to keep pace with them.

And, there was no question that I had to do so. Not that Rhiheto was playing the melodramatic villain or anything. There was no need. After all, he really didn't have to worry that I was going to run off. How could I? Where would I go? We had to be well over a hundred miles from Quito. Even if I could somehow get back down the mountain without breaking my neck, without food or water I knew damn well I wouldn't last as long as one of Vincenzo's diets.

No, Rhiheto had me right where he wanted me. Not that he needed me. After all, he had the ants. Once they had started marching, like I said, they might have reduced their numbers, but they didn't let us lose sight of them—or visa versa. Hell, when we finally stopped for the night the damn things stopped with us. While Rhiheto's men pitched camp, I watched as the ants did the same, settling into a ring around us.

Fascinated and curious, as well as a bit frightened, I walked over to the edge of the ring while we still had a touch of daylight and made a closer inspection of our six-legged guide dogs. Now, I don't make any claims to knowing all that much about bugs outside of the fact I hate finding them in my kitchen, I was surprised by what I found. Surrounding us seemed odd enough. Christ, the fact they were leading us somewhere was odd, their stopping to wait for us was positively bizarre. But, the way they were waiting for us truly freaked me out.

I didn't expect them to start digging new homes for an overnight stay or anything, but I did think they'd be foraging for something to eat. They weren't. In fact, they weren't moving at all. As I bent to get a closer look in the fading light, I saw that not only were they not eating, or scratching or doing anything, but they were doing it in formation. I rubbed my eyes to make sure I was seeing what I thought I was seeing, and I was. The ants had settled into precise columns, all of them staring forward outward into the jungle.

At least at first.

"What are you doing, my friend?" I pointed downward, saying;

"Just checking out our little friends."

"Yes, I noticed earlier. They are waiting for us. Like loyal watch dogs, no?"

I was about to agree, when suddenly, the ants closest to me began to turn. First their heads, then their bodies. Just the one closest to me. Then the ones to its left and right. Then the one behind it. Then the ones to its left and right, and the ones to the first three's lefts and rights. The longer I stared, the larger the pyramid formation continued to grow. Watching the ants move from over my shoulder, Rhiheto suggested;

"Perhaps, maybe, we should leave our little friends be for now. We need our rest, and they need theirs."

I nodded, not saying anything, merely walking away quietly all the while keeping one eye on our tiny companions. The further back into the camp I moved, the more the ants returned to their original positions. I have to admit I found that I'd been holding my breath the whole time. When I exhaled, I actually had to steady myself as a wave of dizziness passed over me.

Of course, I told myself, such a thing was normal. I'll admit that I'm not in the world's greatest shape. On top of that, I'd made a hard walk up the side of a mountain. Not only was I tired from that exertion, but I was a lot higher above sea level than I'm used to. Such things would make anyone short of breath.

But, I also have to admit I didn't think any of that was the cause of my slight attack. I was feeling pan-icked, and I knew it. And I knew why.

The whole thing with the ants leading us through the jungle had been goddamned spooky enough. Then ringing our camp for whatever reason, that was double creepy. But, when just that first one turned around, turned around and craned its head upward to look at me--that was the moment my blood had chilled over frostier than I've ever experienced before.

Then the next one had joined in, and another and another. My heart had stopped pumping, my nerves went dead, my eyes had frozen in place. Up until that moment, all of the various things that had fallen across my path about this whole affair had certainly seemed strange. Smile for the Golden Morning and his weird little lecture, as well as the dreams that had followed. This notion about the seventy-two, coming at me from all sides, and the pair of armies getting ready to fight for lost treasure or weapons or whatever it was being protected by whatever the seventy-two were ... throw all of it together and it raised the weird ante plenty. But then, it all came together.

One of the actual seventy-two was thrown into the mix without me knowing it. His presence not only affected the dreams I was having, but it also delivered the ants to us. When we had first seen the overwhelming rows of them, a part of me had hoped they might be a defense of some sort, a diversion, sent by some higher power to lead us in the wrong direction, to make certain whatever was in this lost city of Rhiheto's never fell into his hands. It had been part of the reason I'd gone along with the drug lord in the first place.

Why not, I'd thought. What difference did it make?

After all, everything of a supernatural nature that had come up connected to this thing had been trying to warn me off, to send me away from the seventy-two. It made perfect sense that the ants would be a part of it as well. Just another bit of strange sent to muddy the waters.

And then, one of them had turned around and looked at me—*stared* at me.

It had not moved as an insect, but as a messenger from something beyond. And in that moment when my eyes locked with that horrible insect gaze, I finally saw everything clearly, realized there was more than one force at work around us… that there was more than one objective being sought.

And that we were all—assuredly—hiking our way into nightmare.

CHAPTER FIFTEEN:

The next morning, as soon as we were ready to move out, the ants formed up their lines and began moving up the side of the mountain once more. I sat on a fallen tree trunk and simply stared at them. I had not washed up the night before, and couldn't bring myself to bother then. Not that anyone else had bothered much. The heat of the jungle, coupled with its stifling humidity even at our current altitude, made the effort fairly useless. I knew I was getting fairly ripe, but I didn't care. What, after all, was the point?

What did it matter—considering?

"Senor Kolchak," asked Rhiheto with a bit too much energy for the early morning, "are you ready for the day's journey? Are you ready to see the city of the seventy-two?"

I stared at the drug lord for a moment, considering my options. Considering that the choices before me were severely limited, it didn't take me long to finish. Tilting my head upward, I caught Rhiheto's eyes and answered;

"I need to ask you something." So saying, I laid out my concerns about the ants as quickly as I could. Smiling, the drug lord told me;

"I will not argue the possibility. Anything, as we know, is possible in this world. Could you be right in this idea of yours? Yes... of course. But, will that possibility stop me this morning...?"

His voice trailed off with a questioning tone, letting me know he expected me to give him an answer. Sighing, I forced myself to my feet, wiping at the sweat on my forehead with the palm of my hand as I told him;

"No, I suppose it won't."

And that, as they say, was that. Sure, I could have argued more, but I could see it would be useless. There had been a look in Rhiheto's eyes I've seen too many times in the past. And, I don't mean since I started running into the Chiller Theater end of the news back in Vegas. No, this was something I'd seen long before that fun-filled moment.

It was that shining quality that sneaks into the corners of the eyes of people who think they have it made. The politician who believes he's untouchable, the gambler who knows the next toss of the dice is going to make his fortune, the woman who's sure that she's finally come up with the way to act and speak that will keep some slob she's tied herself to from beating her senseless that night. It was the unbreakable glow of those that have learned to kid themselves so completely there's no way to show them the truth. If I hadn't already been worried, when I saw that tinge settling over his eyes, I certainly would have started.

Watching the drug lord's men get ready for that day's march let me know things were going to come to a head soon. Whether he was right or not, it was certain he believed we were close. Two of the tents were left standing, and a lot of supplies were moved into them with four of his crew left behind to guard it all. It was obvious Rhiheto believed we were in striking distance of the city, that he wanted his men traveling light. Weapons and ammo were almost all that was being taken. The amount of food and water being packed out wouldn't cover us for a full day.

I had just enough time to figure that much out and then we were on the move again. Three men had been set out on point, all of them several hundred yards apart from each other. Although the ant trails had reduced to a trickle earlier once we had finally taken note of them, when Rhiheto split his front line, the ants did the same, providing each of the point men with a stream of bodies. The sight of it made the drug lord laugh out loud. I had a different reaction myself.

We traveled for several hours, moving upward at a slow, but steady pace. Rhiheto was so confident we had to be close to the city by that point he had his men moving as quietly as possible. Talking was not permitted. He'd even instituted a ban on smoking, which had more than a few of them sweating a bit extra. Neither ban had me very upset. I gave up smoking what seems like a lifetime ago. As for the silence, I knew nothing I said was going to make any difference to the drug lord. I'd tried just before we'd set out that morning—one last attempt to get across to him that we were headed into trouble—but he wasn't hearing it.

He didn't say much to me, only gave me the smile a parent does when their child is afraid of the dark. But, he gave it to me in place of another look. When I had tried to explain to him about the ants, about what I was feeling, a dark hardness had settled in the back of his eyes, scowling outward at me. He had covered it over quick enough, but I saw all I needed of it to know that there was no debating where we going, or what we were going to do.

From the amount of times since Vegas that I've tried to warn people not to do things that they've gone ahead and done anyway, you'd think I'd learn. Seriously, if I ever have a daughter I'm going to name her Cassandra.

According to my watch we had left our previous evening's campsite at 6:33. We had then moved further upward into the mountains at a fairly steady clip for a little over four hours, coming to a stop at 10:41. Rhiheto had received a message from one of his point men via the headsets they were using that there was some sort of commotion going on ahead. We slowed our advance to a crawl while the pointmen moved forward to investigate the noise.

Marsha, who had been getting random footage throughout the morning, taking as many shots of the ants as she did our traveling companions, perked up for the first time. I could see in her eyes that she was ready to film whatever came next, no matter how much blood or mayhem it involved. She was young and hungry and brimming over with the need for that "story of stories." No matter what came next, or how hard it came at us, she was ready to get it all stored and ready for a special report with her by-line on it.

I looked at her for a long moment, wondering just when it was that I'd lost that hunger. Don't get me wrong, I wasn't thinking any noble thoughts at that moment. But, I did realize something that I hadn't before. I had reached a point where I didn't mind covering the flower show, or the public hearing to determine if this or that city ordinance should be reviewed. I could see in not only the look in her eye, but in the way she was crouched, eager to move forward, in the way she was suddenly holding her camera up and away from her shoulder—despite having carried it for hours—that she was ready to catch every moment of blood and thunder that was ahead of us.

I stopped then, sinking to the ground. I sat in the thinner vegetation of the high jungle and closed my eyes as my brain flashed a thousand images through my head, memory after memory of men and women being torn apart, dried out, burned alive, crushed to death, split open—all of it. And with each death I'd witnessed, or body I'd come across, my memories reminded me of just how eager I'd been to follow the trails of blood before me to the next big story, the byline of my own that would make up for the past, propel me back to the public spotlight, reinvent me—finally.

Until that moment, sweating in the jungle, I hadn't actually realized exactly how much death I'd come across, how many bodies I'd photographed, how much carnage I'd witnessed and ignored, all so I could aggrandize myself. Build my reputation. Let the world know how great and wonderful I was compared to everyone else within it. And, the thing that hit me the hardest in that moment was that such episodes had started long before Vegas.

My specialty had been crime. When I had been one of the big dogs, I'd clawed my way to the top of the kennel by covering thieves and killers from both sides of the law. The images flooded my mind, the photos I'd taken of mutilated prostitutes, slaughtered families, revenge killings, drive-by-shootings, terrorist attacks, knifings, shootings, bombings, rivers of blood, lakes of scarlet, all of it propelling me forward—

Then, I suddenly realized, I wasn't actually re-membering everything storming through my brain, something was flashing the cascade of memories through my mind for me. As that notion hit me, I saw Smile for the Golden Morning's face, watched his lips move as he said once more;

"The seventy-two ... must always be."

And then, I felt a touch at my shoulder. As I opened my moist eyes, blinking hard, I saw Rhiheto's joyous face, heard him telling me;

"Come, Senor Kolchak, come. This is the mo-ment. The seventy-two ... we have found them!"

CHAPTER SIXTEEN:

Bak challa challa challa, Bak challa challa challa ...
As we peered out through the trees, we saw seventy-two men sitting on the ground chanting, cross-legged, thirty-six of them on either side of a well-worn pathway. Facing one another, each group took their turn, one after another, pointing their hands upward, aiming their arms over the heads of the fellows, throwing out their chant.

Bak challa challa challa, Bak challa challa challa ...
Outside of the fact they all appeared to be locals, and that they were all males, the seventy-two seemed to have little in common. They were all ages, all sizes. Many of them were bald, or balding, but not all. Some were tattooed, but none in the same fashion, and not all that many of them, either. They wore no specific uniform of any kind. Some wore nothing at all. They did, however, have one thing in common—their eyes.

Bak challa challa challa, Bak challa challa challa ...
There was something in their eyes, a common focus... an unblinking gaze that looked like it was reaching far beyond normal sight. That one fact assured me that this seventy-two was the one we were looking for, and that somewhere on the other side of the path they were guarding was the city everyone wanted to reach. From the look I saw in Rhiheto's

eyes, it was obvious he felt the same way. With a quick set of hand motions he sent ten of his men forward. Heavily armed, they headed down the beaten trail without question.

To their credit, none of them started shooting unarmed men simply because they could. They merely moved forward, watching the seventy-two carefully, as well as the jungle around them. The men on the ground continued to chant as if they had not even noticed those approaching. And then, it happened. The first of the drug lord's men reached the edge of the path bordered by the seventy-two. Propelled by the confidence of their weapons, the pair stepped forward... ready to march through to the other side, only to find they could not.

As the rest of us stared, the first two men struggled vainly to keep walking, but to no avail. As the next few hit the same spot, they tried to move on as well, but had no better luck. Before long, all ten were straining against some unseen barrier, unable to find their way past it. Spreading out, the men moved off the path in both directions, but could not find any spot where they could get through to the other side.

Rhiheto sent more men... then joined the effort himself, but nothing changed. They could not break down whatever wall they had reached. They could find no way around the seventy-two. Then, to complicate matters, shooting broke out in the jungle behind us. It took only seconds to figure out what was happening. Lenzano's forces had found the entrance as well.

At the first sound of gunfire I threw myself behind the largest rock I could find and stayed there. The battle, such as it was, lasted almost ten minutes . I knew that because I had the presence of mind to check my watch. I also knew that no matter how loud the fighting got between the two drug lord's forces, the seventy-two never reacted. Not one of them stopped chanting. Not one of them even looked up. I wasn't the only one who noticed.

When the two forces had come across each other, the first few minutes had been a slaughter with everyone basically out in the open. Quickly scrambling for cover, however, both sides found shelter behind trees and the such, and then threw lead and grenades at each other. Finally, Rhiheto had gotten his forces to stop throwing away ammunition, and had been able to get the other side to do the same.

Always a showman, Rhiheto had insisted Lenzano and he speak in English for the benefit of their media escorts. In a move that I have to admit took real courage, the drug lord had stepped out from concealment, insisting that their two sides needed to talk, and to do so quickly. Impressed by his nerve, the head of the Lenzano forces did the same.

"So speak," said the other side's chief as he marched boldly into the open. "What is it we need to discuss?"

"Did you see when we tried to pass the seventy-two? Did you see?"

The Lenzano man hemmed and hawed for a moment, not wanting to admit to the impossibility he had witnessed, but in the end he relented. As he and Rhiheto drew closer to one another, they argued over the insanity of it all, but with their truce of necessity in place, they moved forward to the edge of the seventy-two together, and the Lenzano chief saw for himself—there was no passing the two squares of chanting men.

"These are not gods," snapped the Lenzano man, finally. "They are but men. And eventually ... men grow tired."

"I agree," answered Rhiheto, "but what if there are more? We had one of them, left him behind. But there are seventy-two out there. Who knows how many replacements they have? Who knows how far away they are? What weapons they might possess? What additional magicks?"

The two leaders looked at each other for a moment, deciding something between them. All around, their men stared at each other, at their bosses, and at the seventy-two. I caught sight of Shibley and Logan, both of whom appeared to have been treated no worse than Marsha and myself. Indeed, they both seemed eager to see what was going to happen next. Myself, I've been around this stuff for too long. I knew what was coming next.

Raising their weapons, both of the leaders turned them toward the invisible barrier and fired. Their bullets were turned away, or more precisely, they were robbed of their momentum. As soon as the slugs hit the barrier, they hung in the air for a moment vibrating, then finally fell to the ground. The two men fired again, and then again, only to have the same thing happen.

Rather than being disheartened by the results, however, if anything, each of them felt insulted. Calling forth their forces, they instructed all of their men to attack the wall with everything they had. For over a minute—almost two—the magic of the seventy-two held back the terrible force being thrown against it. But, only for two.

Watching the chanting men on the other side of the barrier, I saw them begin to sweat, to weaken. Their arms began to appear too heavy for them to hold over their heads. Their voices grew thin, their volume diminished. One after another, the squatting men began to tremble, their eyes glazing, bodies stricken with the shakes. And then, as I knew it would, that first bullet broke through the barrier.

It was a slight thing, a minor triumph only in that it managed to fall to the ground on the other side of the unseen wall, but it was enough. In seconds scores more had fumbled their way through, and then, the barrier was shattered. The chanting men began to be struck by the drug lords' bullets, knocked down... slain without mercy. Before either of the bosses could call for a cease fire, the damage was done. The seventy-two had been annihilated. Their barrier had been shattered.

And, no matter what secret had been kept from mankind since the beginning of time, whatever it was that lie hidden around the corner of the jungle wall at the end of the path, it was now fair game for Rhiheto and Lenzano.

I remained sitting on the ground where I had hidden earlier. Whatever was down the trail, I'd find out sooner or later. I had no interest. What could it matter?

All around me, the drug lords' men raced forward along with their bosses and my colleagues. I watched them as they ran, looked into their faces. The childlike Christmas morning wonder I saw there made me chuckle to myself. Ten minutes earlier most of those streaming past me had been trying to murder one another. Then they had banded together to murder a group of innocents. Now, their carnage forgotten, they all raced forward, laughing, leaping over the bodies of the seventy-two, splashing their way through the blood soaking into the ground.

I reached that stage in any insane string of laughter when the joke is lost and my amusement at the horror all around me subsided. I felt myself slipping over into tears, was grateful for the release.

Then, the first screams started, tearing through the blistering afternoon, and no matter how bad things had seemed, I knew they had just gotten worse.

CHAPTER SEVENTEEN:

I pushed myself to my feet, my mind rolling over a thousand possibilities of what had gone wrong now. What had they found? What nightmare had the seventy-two been protecting the rest of us against for however many centuries they'd been sitting there? The screams coming from down the trail were some of the most terrified I've ever heard, and I've heard plenty.

Over the stinking two years since I'd seen my first vampire, I've come across more hell crap than anyone could imagine. I've seen people pulled apart by monsters on the land, under the water, and in the air. I've watched folks be eaten, crushed and even dissolved. Men, women, old, young, I've witnessed death cries of every possible description. Or at least, I thought I'd had.

What I was hearing coming from down the trail were the most horrified screams imaginable. The sound of them echoed that those trapped just beyond my sight knew they were not merely about to die, but that they were damned as well. And then, the gunfire had begun. When I heard the first shots, they came as a surprise, my mind asking what had taken so long.

After a few moments, I understood. I was not hearing rapid fire. The thugs who had finally remembered they were armed weren't trying to kill whatever they had discovered ... they were killing themselves.

After several minutes of screams and suicide all noise slowly drifted away to be followed by a long period of silence. Having stood up, I remained standing, simply staring down the trail, waiting to see what horror was going to finally come crawling forth to end my miserable life. I didn't try to run. I could tell from the utter despair in the screams I'd been hearing that there was no escaping whatever Rhiheto and the others had found. And to tell the truth, I didn't care. A man can only take so much disappointment in his life before hanging onto every possible second starts to sound like a waste of time.

Finally, after I don't know how long, something moved in the distance. As I watched, sweat pouring down over my forehead, stinging my eyes, one of the thugs stumbled into view. He seemed dazed, his body language that of a beaten man. He was followed by others. Some still possessed their weapons, most didn't. Not that it mattered. Those still armed seemed only to be holding their weapons because they had forgotten how to drop them. Then suddenly, I saw Marsha coming around the corner.

She looked like the others. Frightened. Shrunken. Destroyed.

I began moving forward toward her, reaching out to help her, to ask what had happened, when the next utterly unexpected thing happened. The surviving thugs began to clear away the bodies of the seventy-two, moving them outside the area they had been occupying so they might take their place.

"Bernstein!"

Marsha reacted slightly to the sound of her name, but only slightly. As she began to sit down in one of the spots previously held by one of the seventy-two, I finally snapped out of my stupor and started moving faster. Running to Marsha, I knelt down next to her, shaking her shoulders as I shouted;

"Marsha—what happened? What's going on? What the hell did you find up there?"

She turned her head at an odd angle, her eyes working to focus on my face, her brain trying to recall who I might possibly be. Then, her eyes cleared slightly, and she said;

"Carl. I ... you ... I remember ..."

"What was it? What could be so horrible—"

"No. Not horrible. Not horrible at all. No ..." her voice trailed off for a moment, then she whispered, "beautiful."

As she said the word slowly, drawing it out, her face transformed at the thought of whatever she had encountered, all around us the minions of the two drug factions filled in the seats of those they had slain. They were shaken men, badly scared, many of them weeping openly. I noticed Rhiheto among them, awkwardly settling himself to the ground. As I stared at him, at the overwhelming horror reflected in his eyes, Marsha spoke again, telling me;

"So beautiful ..."

"What's so beautiful," I asked her. Holding her roughly, forcing her face to within a few inches of mine, I shouted, "What did you see? What's coming out of there?"

"Not coming. She never comes. All come to her. But ... too early. Not ready for her. Not yet."

I won't pretend I understood what she meant. I did find myself calming somewhat, however. Marsha was right; nothing seemed to be coming around the corner except those few stragglers remaining of the invading force. I tried to get her to say more, to stand up, but to no avail. While I was concentrating on her, all around me the seventy-two had been reformed.

Suddenly I noticed that all the dead bodies had been removed. Also, all of the well-worn spots where the seventy-two had seated themselves over the centuries were filled once more. Many of the spots had been taken by the would-be invaders. Some were taken by members of the seventy-two who had been there when we had first arrived. One was taken by a green-eyed Jewish reporter who showed no interest in being anywhere but where she was.

The rest of the spots were filled with new faces, bench warmers for the team, I supposed. Before I could make heads or tails out of anything, they were all lifting their arms to the sky as their eternal chant began anew—

Bak challa challa challa, Bak challa challa challa ...

And, once more, the seventy-two were seated on the ground where they belonged, chanting, cross-legged, thirty-six of them on either side of the well-worn pathway. As always.

I made an attempt to move forward, to drag Marsha to her feet, but I couldn't reach her. The same invisible force which had restrained the drug lords' men earlier now held me back as well. How long I fought it, I'm not certain. I only know I did so until I heard a faint voice whispering to me on the wind—

"The seventy-two ... must always be."

And then, I simply sat down, staring at the seventy-two, not knowing what else I could do.

EPILOGUE:

When evening came I was led to the local village which was a kind of support facility for the seventy-two. There, two of the older fellows, men of the world who had gone down from the mountain in their time and learned a thing or two, took turns filling me in on what had happened.

Little was known about that which existed at the end of the trail. Some thought it was a god, or a goddess, the creator of all things ... no one knew for certain. The one thing all could agree on was that whatever it was, it was beautiful. Not the beauty of a succubus, an external glory used to lure the helpless to their doom. No, this thing gave off a subtle loveliness—it was... the radiance of truth.

The thing residing in the mountains was... the embodiment of plain, unvarnished truth, a mirror that apparently mortals simply aren't ready yet to look upon. As the two old timers explained it, most people spend their lives kidding themselves, justifying, rationalizing, making themselves feel better. After a lifetime of avoiding the truth at every turn, most people can't bear the sight of their own souls shown to them. Especially not when it's being reflected back to them from a surface utterly spotless. Seeing the totality of their lives measured against pure truth, the

121

outcome was as I had seen—denial, madness, slaughter. Those that couldn't stand the truthful measure of their lives had ended them. Those that felt they might possibly be able to make up for their sins had taken a seat and began praying.

After the old timers had gotten all of that across to me, it seems I went a little mad myself. Apparently I spent the next three days laughing to myself. When I was told this, I was assured that I had also been running quite a high fever, and that I shouldn't feel too badly about the minor breakdown. I asked if the fever might be responsible for some of what I remembered them telling me. No such luck.

My napmate from much earlier had made his way back to home base. When he and I assured the others that a great deal of supplies were to be had down the mountain, he led the locals back to Rhiheto's last base camp and killed his men quite easily, then took the supplies. The support team of the seventy-two then disappeared back up the mountain with everything, leaving me in the hands of my napmate who, after some nine days travel, managed to get me safely returned to Quito.

From there I had returned to Los Angeles to try and find a story those waiting for me might believe. Incredibly, I found them more willing to believe what I had to tell them than I might have dared.

It seemed that at the same time Rhiheto and Lenzano's forces were battering away at the barrier created by the seventy-two's chanting, minor disruptions were felt around the world. Minor earthquakes which only damaged a single structure, tiny tornadoes that only ripped apart one building, over and over, on every continent, during the same handful of minutes, disasters struck. And, it began to be noticed by those who like puzzles, in every single case, the number seventy-two seemed to play some role.

Like the Korean groceries which just happened to have seventy-two fruit and vegetable bins. Or the Buddhist temple in Hollywood, where the monks made certain that there were always seventy-two candles blazing.

Those who made a game of searching out these coincidental tragedies were able to find slightly over 5,000 such incidents. In case you were wondering, seventy-two times seventy-two comes to 5,184.

The State Department was happy enough with the results. They thanked me for my story, then released their own of untrustworthy drug kingpins and the slaughter of innocent American media personalities. That one was a homosexual and a black, and another, a woman, was emphasized repeatedly. I was asked if I wouldn't mind claiming I didn't accompany those who didn't return up into the mountains. I had been feverish, after all.

I told them "sure." Anything for Uncle Sam.

And there it is, the whole sad story. What happened, I don't actually know. I did have a fever, and I did suffer a bit of a breakdown there in the jungle. What really sits around the corner there in the mountains, I have no idea. How the seventy-two formed, how they ended up with helper units all around the globe, how lighting candles or cleaning carrots could help create a force field thousands of miles away, how any of it ties together, your guess is as good as mine. What took control of those damn ants, what made me keep having visions, what took me to the dreamplane ... again, you figure it out, you tell me.

As for myself, I asked Vincenzo to let me cover every boat and train and flower show that comes our way. Gay Pride parades, city council meetings, firemen rescuing kittens from trees, whatever calm, routine, quiet news rolls along, that's the beat I told him I would happily cover.

You see, I missed a chance to know the complete and utter truth about myself. Those that got that chance either blew their own brains out, or they willingly offered the remainder of their lives in service to the ideal of that exacting knowledge.

As a newsman, I'd always thought my life had been a constant search for the truth.

Now, I'm not so sure.